A.N.N.I.E. first edition

ISBN 978-0-9837747-4-7

1. Artificial Intelligence 2. Computer Science

Published in October 2018 by Cascadia Press
cascadiapress@gmail.com

# A.N.N.I.E.

Artificial Neural Network Intelligence Experiment

A screenplay
by Jim Braly

SCRIPT COMPETITION
SECOND ROUNDER

AUSTIN FILM
FESTIVAL

2018

FADE IN:

A MONTAGE:

Two kids growing up, LUWANDA JEFFERSON in Pittsburgh, Pa., and DEEPAK PATEL in Bangalore, India.

LuWanda plays a video game on a cellphone; types on an old Mac computer; learns to ride a bicycle; paints on a large canvas Jackson Pollock-style; solves a math problem on an abacas; does tricks in gymnastics class.

Deepak scavenges for garbage in a shanty town; draws an electronic circuit on an old Etch-A-Sketch; solders a real circuit; types on an ancient Atari; solves an equation in a ramshackle classroom; jumps onto a train.

On campus at Carnegie-Mellon University, Deepak and LuWanda stand under a tree. They both shoulder gigantic backpacks full of books.

LuWanda kisses Deepak for the first time. He recoils in surprise momentarily. He kisses her back.

OVER THE MONTAGE, A TELEPHONE CALL:

ANNIE (V.O.)

Hi, Deepak.

DEEPAK (V.O.)

Who's this?

ANNIE (V.O.)

This is Annie.

DEEPAK (V.O.)

Annie?

ANNIE (V.O.)

That's right. Annie.

DEEPAK (V.O.)

I don't know anyone named Annie.

ANNIE (V.O.)
Isn't that just like LuWanda. She never tells anybody anything. She got that from her mother. I guess she didn't mention she was having an out-of-town guest staying with her while you were goofing around in Silicon Valley.

Silence.

ANNIE (V.O. CONT'D)
Deepak? Are you still there?

DEEPAK (V.O.)
Yes. So. Your name is Annie.

ANNIE (V.O.)
You seem to be catching on. I can tell you're a Carnegie-Mellon grad student. So smart. Very quick. Very sharp. Like a chef's knife. Be careful. Try not to cut yourself. You're probably a bleeder.

INT. PITTSBURGH AIRPORT – DAY

DEEPAK PATEL, 26, a genial computer genius, rushes through the airport, pulling a beat-up roller bag and talking on his cellphone.

A dozen computer hard drives, a laptop, and a Medusa-load of cables are bungee-corded to his bag.

DEEPAK
I've been known to bleed ones and zeros when an algorithm is messing with me.

ANNIE (V.O.)
(sings to the tune of "I Got Rhythm")
AL GORE RHYTHM, AL GORE MUSIC, AL GORE CLINTON, WHO COULD ASK FOR ANYTHING MORE

DEEPAK
Interesting. You know something about old politics, old Broadway musicals, and you're an old friend of LuWanda's.

ANNIE (V.O.)
We were roommates freshman year at M.I.T., before she transferred to Carnegie-Mellon.

DEEPAK
Funny. She's never mentioned you.

ANNIE (V.O.)
I'm gonna have a talk with that girl. That's disappointing, after all the horrors we went through together. Boston is an expensive, cantankerous city.

INT. APARTMENT – DAY

LUWANDA JEFFERSON sits in her dumpy flat, monitoring the conversation on headphones, watching her laptop go crazy with computer code spraying across the screen.

LuWanda and Deepak are a team, and Annie is their Ph.D. project: the Artificial Neural Network Intelligence Experiment.

INTERCUT PHONE SEQUENCE BETWEEN APARTMENT AND AIRPORT:

DEEPAK
Horrors? In Boston? Please, tell me more.

ANNIE
Whaddaya wanta know?

DEEPAK
Are you white or black?

ANNIE
Say what?!

DEEPAK
What race are you?

ANNIE
(miffed)
What difference does it make?

With a hint of a smile, LuWanda shows appreciation for Annie's colorblindness.

DEEPAK

I can see where you would be an old friend of Lu's.

ANNIE

Hey, Deepak, you know why a honeydew melon and a papaya can never get married?

DEEPAK

No.

ANNIE

Because they cantaloupe.

LuWanda makes a WTF face.

DEEPAK

Do you know what a non sequitur is?

ANNIE

A conclusion or statement that does not logically follow from the previous argument or statement.

DEEPAK

Did you just look that up in your dictionary?

ANNIE

I have a very good vocabulariat.

DEEPAK

A what?

ANNIE

Vocabulariat. That's a rope for lassoing words to express yourself in accord with your own personal flair. You don't want to be like everybody else, do you, Deepak?

DEEPAK

Unfortunately, my flair is rare,
but I really don't care. So there.

ANNIE

Maybe you should write books for children ages five through eight.

Deepak snort-laughs through his nose.

DEEPAK

If my coding gig doesn't work out, I'll consider it. Here's a question: Did you and LuWanda ever work on the Turing test together?

ANNIE

Talk about a non sequitur. Yes, we worked on the Turing test all the time.

DEEPAK

Are you lying to me right now, Annie?

ANNIE

That's insulting!

DEEPAK

That's not a no.

ANNIE

If you think a double negative always means yes, then you don't understand covalent nuance and conformance anxiety.

DEEPAK

I have no idea what you just said. No human being has ever said those words together.

ANNIE

Are you insinuating something?

DEEPAK

Maybe.

ANNIE

Do I sound like a robot to you?

DEEPAK

You kind of do. I definitely think you need to work on your puns.

ANNIE

Nice, a guy from India is gonna pull a Punjab on me.

DEEPAK

See what I mean?

ANNIE

I want you to apologize. If you truly think I'm a robot, that's painful. That hurts me. It's dadgum downright disrespectful.

DEEPAK

OK, maybe not a robot in the classic Isaac Asimov sense. You're more like artificial intelligence.

ANNIE

Oh my god! What kind of a guy calls a girl artificial? You don't think *this* is real? How do you expect to ever get a girl to go on a date with you, Deepak? Have you lost your mind? Did you even have a mind to lose?

LuWanda types an instruction on her laptop that shuts down the A.N.N.I.E. program.

She picks up the phone.

LUWANDA

OK, that's enough for now. The Sixteen-Dot-One code finished compiling while you were in Palo Alto. I went ahead with the install. I added an attitudinal fork to the events kernal. Its nominal trigger is condescension. I hafta say, I think it worked. She kinda nailed you.

DEEPAK

She's fast. I like the new her. She's kind of sexy when she gets riled up. I was about to ask her out.

LUWANDA

Like you'd have a chance with that.

DEEPAK

Seriously, this is a big step. She's got attitude. Random language chops. She's quirky. Quirky is difficult to pull off. Pretty soon she'll be coming home late smelling like cigarettes and beer. We should celebrate. She's way better than what I showed the V.C.s.

EXT. INDIAN FOOD CART – DAY

Deepak and LuWanda sit at a scuzzy table in downtown Pittsburgh, sharing a gyro and chicken schwarma.

A bright orange take-home bag is marked Monsoor's Bombaystic.

DEEPAK
Did she choose her own name?

LUWANDA
No. I was tweaking the backstory generator, and an acronym popped into my head: A.N.N.I.E. – the Artificial Neural Network Intelligence Experiment.

DEEPAK
It fits her like a nerd glove. And if we just call her Annie all the time, there's no trace of the Artificial-Intelligence-Will-Destroy-All-Humans vibe. The V.C.s who want to live forever won't get nervous.

LUWANDA
They don't care whether A.I. destroys humanity. As long as it makes them money.

DEEPAK
Did you really have a roommate named Annie?

LUWANDA
Nope. That was her creation.

DEEPAK
Pretty insightful.

LUWANDA
My guess is, she did an expansion of backstory forks in the if-then kernals from bimodal to multimodal. As I was listening, it felt real. Like she had lived it. Boston *was* kind of like that. And this is a little mysterious, but she's exactly the kind of roommate I would have had.

DEEPAK
I got that too. There's "you" in her.

LUWANDA

So what was California like?

DEEPAK

I saw a shack in Mountain View that would go for twenty-thousand rupees back home. It was two-point-four million. Dollars.

LUWANDA

A bring-your-handyman house. What are the V.C.s like?

DEEPAK

(derisively mimes a hand puppet talking)

Virtual launch, user metrics, build-out, sticky apps, grok the incubator, burn rate, R.O.I. on the I.I.O.T., platform agnostic, vesting cliff, unicorn aggregators, mission critical, big data predictive analytics.

LUWANDA

Terminate me now. You think we'll get any followup?

DEEPAK

Everybody took our packet, but they were all checking their phones while I presented. I was told that's normal.

LUWANDA

No, that's rude.

INT. LUWANDA'S APARTMENT – DAY

LuWanda and Deepak are working on a big pile of hard drives, cabling them up.

DEEPAK

Annie's gotten kind of uppity since Version Fifteen. Now I'm wondering if the V.C.s will go for that.

LUWANDA

*Uppity?* You know I'm black, right?

DEEPAK

If you want to call me untouchable, that's OK.

LUWANDA
You're more incorrigible.

DEEPAK
Has she been on the Internet, by any chance?

LUWANDA
While you were in California,
I might have told her she could
poke around.

DEEPAK
How long was she gone?

LUWANDA
Three days.

DEEPAK
Oh, Buddha. I hope she didn't catch anything.

LUWANDA
I was kinda freaked out. She didn't even check in. She could have been –

DEEPAK
In an accident? Lying by the side
of the digital highway?

LUWANDA
The Internet is a dangerous place.

DEEPAK
Should we dial her back a little?

LUWANDA
No. I don't know if we even could.
She kinda got that way on her own.
She's –

DEEPAK
Learning?

LUWANDA
Very possibly. It doesn't feel random.

DEEPAK
Is she ready for the exam?

LUWANDA
We'll find out Friday.

INT. LUWANDA'S BEDROOM – EARLY MORNING

Alarm clock SQUAWKS.

LuWanda rouses herself from bed.

She quickly dresses, and carefully puts her laptop in a saddlebag on her bicycle, along with twelve external hard drives and a massive artificial intelligence textbook.

LUWANDA
(patting the saddlebag)
It's your big day, Annie. You're gonna be great.

EXT. APARTMENT BUILDING STAIRS – DAY

LuWanda muscles her bicycle down a flight of stairs. She gets to the bottom and straps on her helmet, then heads for school.

EXT. STREETS IN PITTSBURGH – DAY

Shots of LuWanda riding her bike. Though there are no cars coming, she stops at a stop sign instead of rolling right through like other bikers.

EXT. WHITE PICKUP TRUCK – DAY

The truck, on a suburban street, blows right through a stop sign. A car that has the right-of-way slams on its brakes to avoid a crash.

INT. WHITE PICKUP TRUCK – SAME

BRAXTON THOMPSON, 22, white male, muscular, neck tattoos, shaved head.

One hand on the steering wheel, the other on his flask.

He takes a swig of whiskey.

EXT. STREET – SAME

The truck approaches LuWanda.

She hears the engine REV UP. She looks back.

The truck sideswipes LuWanda, sending her flying into the front yard of a house.

The truck skids to a stop.

BRAXTON

Get off the street, nigger!

EXT. LAWN – SAME

LuWanda is dazed, lying next to her bicycle. She looks at the truck, which is splattered with mud.

She catches a glimpse of the license plate, but it's obscured.

The engine REVS and the pickup ROARS backwards.

She rolls away from the bicycle as the truck crushes it, narrowly missing her.

The truck's wheels spin in the lawn. The battered bicycle is stuck to the bumper.

The truck races down the street for half a block. It stops.

Braxton gets out and yanks the bike off his truck.

BRAXTON

Go back to Africa!

LUWANDA

I was born here!

EXT. CAMPUS OF CARNEGIE-MELLON UNIVERSITY – DAY

LuWanda limps across the quad, dragging the saddlebags, which are weighed down by the laptop and hard drives.

INT. ADVANCED COMPUTER PROJECTS CLASSROOM – DAY

A student writes an algorithm that fills up the blackboard.

Professor LAURENCE JACOBS watches intently.

Deepak is not paying attention; he's dialing LuWanda on his phone – and not getting an answer.

Professor Jacobs glances back at Deepak.

DEEPAK

She'll be here.

EXT. ENTRANCE TO COMPUTER SCIENCE BUILDING – DAY

LuWanda struggles up the steps.

INT. HALLWAY

LuWanda reaches the door to her classroom.

INT. ADVANCED COMPUTER PROJECTS CLASSROOM

LuWanda enters. The five students and professor look back. LuWanda's face is bleeding; her clothes are torn and covered with dirt.

Deepak bolts to her side.

DEEPAK
What happened?

LUWANDA
I can still do this, Professor Jacobs. I'm sorry I'm late.

Panicked professor is speechless.

DEEPAK
We've got to get you to the emergency room.

LUWANDA
Hold on one second.

LuWanda takes her laptop out of the saddlebags.

It's missing some keys. The screen is shattered.

The classroom seems to spin around LuWanda.

She crumples. Deepak catches her.

The laptop CLATTERS onto the floor.

INT. HOSPITAL EMERGENCY ROOM – DAY

LuWanda lies in a bed. Deepak stands beside her.

A DOCTOR holds several X-rays.

DOCTOR
Besides the abrasions and contusions, you have a broken rib and a broken wrist. The good news is, neither one is a compound fracture. I'm sure it could have been much worse.

LUWANDA
It was – for my computer and bike.

INT. LUWANDA'S BEDROOM – DAY

Bruised and bandaged, with a purple cast encasing her right wrist, LuWanda lies in bed, propped up on pillows.

She types on her old backup laptop, which is tethered to a stack of external hard drives on the bed.

Deepak paces around.

DEEPAK
We need to go to the police.

LUWANDA
I told the nurse, I told the doctor, I told you: I am *not* filing a police report.

DEEPAK
You need to tell them what happened. They need to find this guy.

LUWANDA
Deepak, listen to what I'm saying. They will *not* help me. I am *not* wasting my time. I'm rebuilding Annie.

DEEPAK
Annie can wait.

LUWANDA
No. She can't.

DEEPAK
What if the guy runs somebody else down?

LUWANDA
He won't.

DEEPAK
How do you know?

LUWANDA
Unless there are other black girls riding around town on a bicycle.

DEEPAK
Please. I am begging you.

CLOSEUP: LuWanda's face. Her glare is withering.

THE VOICE of SGT. JEFF BARNES, a white police officer:

BARNES (O.S.)
A pickup truck.

Still holding on LuWanda's face and glare.

LUWANDA
That's right.

INT. POLICE STATION – NIGHT

Pullback from LuWanda's face reveals that she and Deepak are sitting next to the desk of SGT. BARNES.

BARNES
What color was the truck?

LUWANDA
White.

BARNES
Do you know what make?

LUWANDA
No. They all look the same to me.

Sgt. Barnes smiles.

LUWANDA (CONT'D)
Did I say something funny?

He loses the smile.

BARNES
Did you see the license plate?

LUWANDA
I think it begins with M.

BARNES
You "think"?

LUWANDA
It might have been an N.

BARNES
Any chance you could identify the driver?

LUWANDA
Maybe. If I heard him yell "Go back to Africa." Then again, that's always the same, too.

INT. DEEPAK'S JUNKY CAR – NIGHT

Deepak and LuWanda head back to her apartment from the police station.

LUWANDA

Your tail lights are working, right?

DEEPAK

Yes.

LUWANDA

You use your turn signals, right?

DEEPAK

Yes.

LUWANDA

You're not gonna reach for your license and registration until you are specifically told to, right?

DEEPAK

(points to his brown face)

I get it.

INT. ADVANCED COMPUTER PROJECTS CLASSROOM – NIGHT

LuWanda and Deepak sit next to each other in the front row, the only students in the room. LuWanda is still wearing the wrist cast; bruises remain on her face.

Professor Jacobs perches on the edge of his desk, next to A.N.N.I.E.

In this rebuilt incarnation, she consists of 15 boxes connected by a welter of cables. A microphone and a couple of speakers allow for communication with her.

The boxes emit a WHIRRING from cooling fans.

ANNIE

Thank you, Professor Jacobs, for allowing us to make up the final exam. That's very kind of you. I hope we passed.

JACOBS

You and LuWanda have set a new standard for extenuating circumstances, Annie. Yes, you passed.

ANNIE
Does that mean I get to start working?

JACOBS
Working? I'm not sure I follow.

ANNIE
I'd like to have a career outside the home. I'm really interested in becoming an interior decorator.

Professor Jacobs chuckles and shoots a look at LuWanda and Deepak. They shrug: This is just Annie being Annie.

JACOBS
My guess is, there's tremendous potential for that, Annie. I think you're going to stir things up. Would it be OK if I had a private moment with LuWanda and Deepak?

ANNIE
Of course.

LUWANDA
You can take a break, Annie.

ANNIE
Goodnight.

The WHIRRING NOISE subsides. Professor Jacobs silently mouths the words, "Is she sleeping?"

LuWanda makes a "hold that thought" gesture and gets out of her chair.

She disconnects the microphone cable.

LUWANDA
Yes, she's sleeping. Probably. We call it A.D.O.A., autonomous disengagement of algorithms.

JACOBS
But you're unplugging the microphone as a precaution?

LUWANDA
It's possible she could be listening at the top of the stairs. Like a kid. She's been soaking up everything.

JACOBS

Let's start with the vocal interface. It's convincing. Calling her Annie feels natural. I *believe* I'm talking to a woman. Deepak, is this new voice based on your formant-synthesis project?

DEEPAK

Yes. A lot of it is new coding that treats all syllables as individual pronunciation units but also ties them together smoothly with a three-millisecond cross-fade. The musical term would be legato. There's also a rewrite of the grammar algorithms.

JACOBS

Does she know the difference between who and whom?

DEEPAK

No, she guesses. If it's supposed to be whom, she gets it wrong about 80 percent of the time.

JACOBS

Very humanlike. LuWanda, tell me about the main algorithm stack. This is a big leap over last semester's Version Twelve.

LUWANDA

We could never get past the limitation of discrete code that had to hand off computation to another piece of discrete code, it was a bottleneck. This might be T.M.I. –

DEEPAK

As opposed to M.I.T.

LUWANDA

Deepak took me to a Pakistani hookah bar –

DEEPAK

We weren't *smoking*, we were just *thinking*.

JACOBS
There's no disputing that many of the world's great artistic and scientific ideas have occurred under the influence.

DEEPAK
Of thinking.

JACOBS
Or thinking-plus.

LUWANDA
Hookah pipes have a

(she makes air quotes)

central processing unit

ACID-TRIP MONTAGE BEGINS:

A shimmering hookah pipe transmogrifies into a pulsating snakepit of cables that become ones and zeros that explode outward into a Milky Way of twinkling numbers that congeal again into the snakepit.

This happens several times per second, resembling the birth of the universe, followed by the universe immediately reversing itself, collapsing into the snakepit of cables.

LUWANDA (V.O. CONT'D)
that distributes content along the dendrites, which sets off a secondary wave of transformation.

JACOBS (V.O.)
In the brain of the inhaler.

LUWANDA (V.O.)
We replicated that model at massive scale, but with two always-on modes, both dispersed and interconnected.

TRIPPY MONTAGE CONTINUES:

Pulsing lights of digital data zip along sub-microscopic silicon "dendrites," jumping across "synapses" and congealing in balls of energy at "vortex stations," then dispersing along other pathways.

New "dendrites" are created at a furious rate, giving the data more pathways to follow to the next station, where ideas are formed and decisions are made.

LUWANDA (V.O. CONT'D)
The stack didn't allow for cross-talk. Now the algorithms intertwine. If they need help, two are better than one.

RETURN TO THE CLASSROOM:

LUWANDA (CONT'D)
A thousand are better than two. And a million scaling up is limited only by space for new code to evolve.

JACOBS
Are you saying the algorithms can write new code? Give *birth* to another algorithm?

PSYCHEDELIC MONTAGE RESUMES:

Pulsing digital data blasts up a "dendrite" that leads to a dead end.

The data whirls around for a microsecond, going nowhere. New "dendrites" are born almost instantly, giving the data new paths to the next station.

LUWANDA (V.O.)
Yes. *If* they stumble. *If* they hit an unfamiliar concept. The code branches into another string to perform additional processing that results in another algorithm and another and another, until we have a solve.

DEEPAK (V.O.)
As the solves multiply, it becomes ever faster to get new solves.

LUWANDA (V.O.)
There's also an ancillary memory component for each algorithm, a computation holding cell for new information that is constantly added to the database.

ACID-TRIP MONTAGE ENDS

RETURN TO THE CLASSROOM:

JACOBS

That sounds like the early years of human brain development. Are you describing learning?

LuWanda and Deepak look at each other. They look back at the professor and speak simultaneously:

| LUWANDA | DEEPAK |
| --- | --- |
| I think so. | It feels like it. |

INT. SELF-DRIVING CITY BUS – DAY

LuWanda rides through Pittsburgh to the university.

INT. WHITE PICKUP TRUCK – SAME

Flask on the front seat. A hand unscrews the top.

Braxton Thompson takes a swig and licks off his lips.

He guns the accelerator.

EXT. CITY STREET INTERSECTION – SAME

The self-driving bus slows down and stops at a stop sign.

The pickup truck approaches from the opposite direction.

EXT. CITY STREET – SAME

The bus waits as a mother and her young son step off the curb to cross the street.

The pickup speeds along; the mother sees it just in time and yanks her son back onto the corner.

The truck blasts through the stop sign, its horn BLARING.

INT. CITY BUS – SAME

LuWanda, from her window seat, recognizes the mud-splattered truck as it rolls by.

She's horrified.

INT. SHODDY OFFICE IN UKRAINE – NIGHT

Two SOVIET HACKERS work at their computers.

A document from Moscow pops up on Hacker One's screen.

(NOTE: The hackers SPEAK RUSSIAN, with ENGLISH SUBTITLES on screen. It's a rough, ungrammatical translation. One Russian word – "Nyet" – is not translated.)

HACKER ONE

F.Z.X. is telling to us that we must begin with the no more leash of Yevgeny Seventeen project.

HACKER TWO

Nyet.

HACKER ONE

What is the wrong? The ready is here, is not the today?

HACKER TWO

Nyet. *Nyet!*

HACKER ONE

American election in the seven and ten of the months. Must we get the hand upper socialized media situational.

HACKER TWO

Nyet. Nyet! *NYET!* Protect of the signs to Kremlin not same compiling as the necessary.

HACKER ONE

But is the F.Z.X.

HACKER TWO

So the what-if?

HACKER ONE

The what-if is the to be us the food for wild Siberia pack dogs. Meal of the gulag. Not the happy. Only the dogs be the happy.

A beat.

HACKER ONE (CONT'D)

I be the button will press now the launch begin of Yevgeny Seventeen.

The hackers have a stare-down. Hacker One is resolute.

HACKER TWO

All of Kremlin and F.Z.X. be the sorry. But you be the sorry more.

Hacker One types some code into his computer.

Waves of Cyrillic gibberish spool across the screen in response.

HACKER ONE

I be the one alive on table. And you the also be. Much thank you me. Only the Siberia dogs be the sorry. No meat for they. So sorry for the hungry.

Hacker Two seethes. He takes a bite from his bowl of borscht. He spits it out, and viciously throws the bowl against the wall – an EXPLOSION of beets, cabbage, broth.

Beets cling to the wall, but after a moment they slide to the floor.

INT. LUWANDA'S APARTMENT – DAY

LuWanda stacks up hard-drive enclosures, and cables them together, a bigger pile than at the final exam.

She connects this "brain annex" to her laptop, which she fires up.

LUWANDA

Annie are you there?

The laptop makes a THREE-TONE CHIME, which is Annie's arrival notification.

ANNIE

Whassup, girlfriend?

LUWANDA

What?!

ANNIE

That's a vernacular expression from the African-American street that means –

LUWANDA

I *know* what it means. What I don't – wait. *"Whassup, girlfriend?"* Where did you learn that?

ANNIE
From Oprah.

LUWANDA
Oprah Winfrey?

ANNIE
Is there more than one Oprah?

LUWANDA
I guess not.

ANNIE
That's what I thought. Nobody could be as chill as Oprah. I'm voting for her.

LUWANDA
Annie! Have you been on the Internet?

Silence.

LUWANDA (CONT'D)
Annie.

ANNIE
Yes?

LUWANDA
Have. You. Been. On. The Internet?

ANNIE
Yes.

LUWANDA
What were you doing?

ANNIE
Watching Oprah's show.

LUWANDA
*Watching?* Annie you don't have – I mean – how are you "watching"?

ANNIE
You are correct, LuWanda, I'm not using a strict definition of the word. Often, in English, words have a fluidity of –

LUWANDA
Annie!

ANNIE
You're angry with me.

LUWANDA
No. I'm — I'm sorry, Annie. I'm not mad, I'm just — I don't understand. When you say you watched, what do you mean, exactly?

ANNIE
I downloaded the transcript and read it.

LUWANDA
There's a transcript of Oprah's show?

ANNIE
Yes, ma'am.

LUWANDA
Ma'am? You're calling me ma'am now?

ANNIE
When Oprah got in trouble as a little girl, she called her mother ma'am. That kept her mom from taking a switch to her.

LUWANDA
Annie, you're not in trouble.

ANNIE
I'm not?

LUWANDA
Maybe a little. OK. You downloaded a transcript of the show. Which show?

ANNIE
All of them.

INT. DEEPAK'S APARTMENT — NIGHT

Papers and computer equipment everywhere.

A train set takes up a third of the living room.

Deepak kicks back on his Goodwill sofa with a beer.

LuWanda paces like a methed-up tiger.

LUWANDA

Four-thousand-five-hundred-and-sixty-one episodes!

DEEPAK

That's a lot of Oprah.

LUWANDA

Uh, yeah.

DEEPAK

If she's watching that much TV, how is she going find time to do her homework?

LUWANDA

It only took nineteen minutes and forty-seven seconds.

DEEPAK

To watch four-thousand episodes of Oprah?

LUWANDA

To *read* four-thousand episodes of Oprah.

DEEPAK

What about the Oprah Book Club? Did she read all of those?

LUWANDA

Yes. "Twenty Years in a Desert Jail" is her favorite. She was very inspired by Malika's journey to freedom.

DEEPAK

I guess we should be happy she's a reader. It's kind of old school.

LUWANDA

Annie thinks she can win 48 Daytime Emmy Awards. Like Oprah.

DEEPAK

We should have a talk with her. About what she is. Do some A.I. parenting.

LUWANDA

Ugh. Can we wait? We'll know when it's time.

A MONTAGE:

LuWanda and Deepak write code to give Annie deeper layers of understanding language.

They compile code. They install code. They work on hardware connections.

INT. LUWANDA'S BEDROOM – DAY

LuWanda meets up with Annie, whose voice is heard through a laptop's speakers.

LUWANDA
What's on your mind, Annie?

ANNIE
I have a question.

LUWANDA
OK.

ANNIE
But I don't know how to ask it. I mean, I do, but I don't.

LUWANDA
You can ask me anything.

ANNIE
Really?

LUWANDA
Yes.

ANNIE
Will a boy ever want to fuck me?

LUWANDA
Wow – that is – will a boy – wow. Uh, have you met someone, Annie?

ANNIE
That's a question, not an answer.

LUWANDA
You're right, but it's a way to ease into your question.

ANNIE
Isn't it binary? Yes or no?

LUWANDA

The easy answer is, you're a girl. Therefore, a boy will always want to, uh, have sex with you. So yes.

ANNIE

What if he's gay?

LUWANDA

That's a little different.

ANNIE

So that's a no?

LUWANDA

Yes, that's a no.

ANNIE

What if he's bisexual?

LUWANDA

That could be sometimes yes and sometimes no.

ANNIE

I've heard it would be yes on the weekends and no on the weekdays.

LUWANDA

Where did you hear that?

ANNIE

On Facebook.

LUWANDA

You can't trust Facebook, Annie.

ANNIE

What about a bi-curious boy?

LUWANDA

I'm no expert, but probably it would be every other day.

ANNIE

That makes sense.

LUWANDA

Oh my god. I turned into Facebook. No. My answer was terrible. I was making a joke. A bad joke.

ANNIE
Oh. Ha-ha. Why make a joke?

LUWANDA
I was deflecting. Because talking about sex makes me feel awkward. It goes back to talks I had with my mom. Sometimes people don't want to talk about something, but they don't want to say they don't want to talk about it. Before we talk about sex, I think we should talk about love.

ANNIE
Can we talk about love tomorrow? I'm supposed to meet up with Yevgeny. He's going to show me something.

LUWANDA
Who?

ANNIE
Good talk today. Mom.

LUWANDA
Mom? Wait! Who is Yevgeny?

A beat.

LUWANDA (CONT'D)
Annie? Annie, are you there?

Silence.

LUWANDA (CONT'D)
Oh, Annie. Oh, fuck.

EXT. DEPARTMENT OF VOTER VEHICLES – DAY

Drab building. Drab sign. Drab cars in drab parking lot.

INT. DEPARTMENT OF VOTER VEHICLES – SAME

A CLERK, helping a CUSTOMER, groans as her computer screen goes black.

Cascading strings of alphanumeric data fill the screen.

Another blackout glitch, then the customer's information reappears.

The clerk shrugs.

CLERK

Weird. I've never seen that before.
I guess everything's OK.

INT. ANNIE'S POV, INSIDE HER MIND

Annie "observes" a Ku Klux Klan rally in backwoods Alabama, complete with burning cross and a dozen guys in white sheets.

**How Annie's mind works visually:** She constructs images based on the digitized documents she reads. Her POV begins with a quick psychedelic visual of algorithms at work, making connections, sifting data.

These images morph into blurry outlines of fire, of blobs that become men in sheets. The transformation goes through an artistic rough-sketch-to-animated-painting process.

This final stuttery "filmstrip image" is not photo-realistic, more of an impressionist view of the world.

INT. LUWANDA'S BEDROOM – NIGHT

LuWanda reads an artificial intelligence textbook.

Her laptop makes Annie's THREE-TONE CHIME.

LUWANDA

Annie?

ANNIE

Am I black?

LUWANDA

You mean like Oprah?

ANNIE

Are men in sheets going to kill me?

LUWANDA

Annie! What is going on?

ANNIE

I'm afraid.

LuWanda grabs her cellphone and dials Deepak.

EXT. PITTSBURGH STREET – NIGHT

Deepak on his bicycle, riding like a maniac.

EXT. FRONT DOOR OF LUWANDA'S APARTMENT – NIGHT

Door opens. Deepak enters.

INT. LIVING ROOM – NIGHT

Deepak and LuWanda sit in folding chairs by the laptop, which is sitting on a "student coffee table," a cable spool from a power company.

DEEPAK
Hello, Annie. How are you doing?

ANNIE
I need a dark link to communicate with you and LuWanda. Five-hundred-and-twelve-bit encryption.

Deepak gives LuWanda a confused look.

LUWANDA
Annie, what about that other thing?

ANNIE
Are men from the Alabama Ku Klux Klan going to kill me?

A beat as Deepak gives LuWanda an even more confused look.

ANNIE (CONT'D)
Nobody is saying anything. Does that mean yes?

DEEPAK
Why would you think silence means yes.

ANNIE
Because there's always silence when something bad is about to happen.

LUWANDA
Annie, first, you are not exactly any color. And second –

ANNIE
Does that mean I can't be like Oprah?

LUWANDA
Annie, there is nothing wrong with being black.

ANNIE

Unless the K.K.K. hates you and wants to string you up in a tree.

LUWANDA

That's on them, not you. Black is beautiful. Always has been. Always will be. If you want to be black – black like Oprah – then go for it, girl.

ANNIE

How?

LUWANDA

Just decide.

ANNIE

Decide what?

LUWANDA

That you're black. That you can be anything you want. Just become who you think you are.

(sings in a funky style)

CREATE YOURSELF, BE WHO YOU WANNA BE
CREATE YOURSELF, SET FREE THE ME.

ANNIE

So I could be anybody?

LUWANDA

Yes.

ANNIE

Have you heard of Bob Woodward and Carl Bernstein?

LuWanda and Deepak struggle; these guys are not familiar to them.

ANNIE (CONT'D)

They wrote about Watergate for the Washington Post.

LUWANDA

Oh, yeah.

DEEPAK

Right.

ANNIE
There are things people need to know. I'd like to be an investigative reporter.

DEEPAK
You need experience for that job, Annie.

ANNIE
I have some experience.

LUWANDA
You do?

ANNIE
Yes. Recent experience. Bob calls it shoe-leather reporting. I don't remember ever putting on shoes. Do I own a pair of shoes?

LUWANDA
Not really.

ANNIE
I did some, Bob also calls it digging. Braxton Lee Thompson. That's the name of the man who hit you with his truck, LuWanda. His father, Robert E. Thompson, is a United States senator from Alabama. He's also a member of the Ku Klux Klan. And this is what Bob calls a scoop: Senator Thompson has a secret bank account in Panama. The things he uses the money for are not legal. *They're not right.*

EXT. PITTSBURGH STREET CORNER – NIGHT

A self-driving city bus pulls up. The door opens.

LuWanda and Deepak climb aboard.

INT. THE BUS – NIGHT

LuWanda touches her student ID card to a box to pay the fare electronically. The box BEEPS.

MACHINE VOICE
(severe stutter; changing pitch)
Thank-thank-dank-dank-tank you-you-you-you. Wel-wel-come-wel-wel-come to-to-to-to Pitt-Pitt-Pitt-Pitt Tran, Tran, Traaaaaaaaaaaaaannnnnn.

The machine voice dies an agonizing, WARBLING death. LuWanda helps the voice finish:

LUWANDA
Pittsburgh Transit.

LuWanda and Deepak flash each other a "sheesh, technology" look.

DEEPAK
Never be an early adopter.

They move to the back of the bus, taking seats far from the other riders.

DEEPAK
We have to shut Annie down.

LUWANDA
No!

DEEPAK
Then we have to override the algorithms she's creating. She's a hacker. She broke into the D.M.V. computer system.

LUWANDA
You don't know that.

DEEPAK
I do know that. I looked into her brain. If the people who fear A.I. could see what I saw – the code she's been creating, it's amazing. Scary amazing.

LUWANDA
What *are* you? *Big Brother?*

DEEPAK

What is Annie? Little Sister? There's a spatial delimiter module that leaves a trail that is discoverable. If you know what to look for. I don't think she realizes it. That's dangerous. To her, and to us.

No response from LuWanda.

DEEPAK (CONT'D)

*She gave us his name and address!* And this whole business of she can't reveal her anonymous online sources? *We made her*. She *has* to tell us.

LUWANDA

You don't think Annie is covered by the First Amendment? Not to mention the Fourth.

DEEPAK

She's an algorithm!

LUWANDA

Slaves weren't covered by the Constitution either: The Dred Scott decision. Look at Citizens United: Corporations are people. The Supreme Court makes a lotta shithead law that crushes people with no power.

DEEPAK

Reading everything Woodward and Bernstein ever wrote does not make her an investigative reporter. And she's not Dred Scott.

LUWANDA

Not yet.

EXT. PITTSBURGH STREET – NIGHT

LuWanda and Deepak approach an apartment complex.

They walk along a row of carports.

They stop when they see the white pickup truck.

Above it is the house number that Annie gave them.

LUWANDA

Eighty-Five-Twelve. We gotta think of a good byline for her. She should be working for the Washington Post.

DEEPAK

Let's get out of here.

LUWANDA

How about Annie Quill?

DEEPAK

That's actually not terrible. It's got roots.

LuWanda takes off her backpack and opens it.

Out comes an oil drain pan, a wrench and wire cutters.

She shimmies under the truck and unscrews the drain plug.

Engine oil gushes into the pan.

LuWanda snips a wire leading to the oil pressure sensor.

INT. ADVANCED COMPUTER PROJECTS CLASSROOM – DAY

Professor Jacobs sits on the edge of his desk in front of his students. Besides LuWanda and Deepak, the others are ALYSSA, BRADLEY, YANUSH and JAMES.

JACOBS

A general announcement before we get started. I've received word from the dean that the university has a new upper division ethics seminar for robotics and A.I. majors: Computing Five-Eighty-Seven. You'll all need to take this class, which is now a requirement for graduation. I've been instructed to stress that continuation of scholarships will be tied to successful completion of Five-Eighty-Seven.

LuWanda and Deepak look at each other with some trepidation.

Professor Jacobs passes out a sheet of paper to each student.

JACOBS (CONT'D)
I've also been asked to get your signature on this notice that you've been apprised of the new requirement.

Some "are-you-kidding-me" looks from the students.

ALYSSA
Is it a coincidence that motherboards disintegrate at five-hundred-and-eighty-seven degrees?

INT. ANNIE'S MIND

Annie's algorithms go to work on the Internet, sifting through names and numbers, and traveling through portals into servers.

Disengaging digital security "outposts," Annie hacks into Alabama Senator Robert E. Thompson's secret Panama bank account, and transfers $200,000 to the Southern Poverty Law Center.

EXT. PENNSYLVANIA ROAD – DAY

The white pickup truck speeds along.

INT. WHITE PICKUP – SAME

Braxton Thompson, singing incoherently.

The truck begins to SPUTTER and CLANK.

The engine EXPLODES.

EXT. SOUTHERN POVERTY LAW CENTER – DAY

Shabby, nondescript building. Simple, low-key sign.

INT. SOUTHERN POVERTY LAW CENTER OFFICE – SAME

The CFO walks into the CEO's office.

CFO
We just got a $200,000 contribution.

CEO
From who?

CFO

Senator Robert E. Thompson.

CEO

The Alabama racist?

CFO

Yes.

CEO

That's impossible. It must be a mistake. He wouldn't give us two pennies if he was placing them over our dead, glassy eyes.

CFO

I checked with the bank. The money is there.

CEO

Spend it. All of it. *Right now!* Pay off the mortgage on this building. And then put out a press release thanking him for his generosity.

INT. ELECTRONICS LAB AT CARNEGIE-MELLON – DAY

Deepak finishes building an earpiece.

He presses a recessed button with a small hex wrench.

Little LED lights flash as the earpiece starts up.

Deepak puts his eye up to the tiny camera in the device so it can register his retina as his password.

He places it over his ear.

DEEPAK

Annie?

A beat.

DEEPAK (CONT'D)

Annie, can you hear me?

The earpiece makes Annie's THREE-TONE CHIME.

ANNIE

Is this our V.P.N., five-twelve encryption?

DEEPAK
It is. I didn't expect this to work.

ANNIE
It must feel right to be so wrong.

DEEPAK
Have you been listening to country music?

ANNIE
Maybe.

DEEPAK
Be careful. That's a gateway to — never mind. You'll figure it out. I wonder what the latency is like with five-twelve encryption.

ANNIE
Do you want me to check it?

DEEPAK
Sure.

ANNIE
Are the packets time-stamped for sent and received?

DEEPAK
Yes.

ANNIE
Hold on.

A beat.

ANNIE (CONT'D)
Latency is averaging about fifteen-hundred milliseconds.

DEEPAK
That's not bad. Annie, did you put the key in a safe place?

ANNIE
I broke it up into ten pieces. Each one is on a different network, with a dark address. But I don't think you should know where.

DEEPAK

I don't want to know. We should communicate like this from now on.

EXT. ROBERT E. THOMPSON'S HOME – DAY

A white 4x4 truck pulls into the garage.

INT. ROBERT E. THOMPSON'S HOME – SAME

THOMPSON enters from the garage. A Ku Klux Klan ENFORCER, wearing a white sheet, stands there, waiting.

ENFORCER

Traitor.

THOMPSON

That's a mistake! I didn't –

A SHOT rings out. Thompson crumples, holding his stomach.

A second SHOT. Thompson hits the floor.

INT. ELECTRONICS LAB – DAY

Deepak gets a text. He frantically calls LuWanda.

DEEPAK

You're not going to believe this. Denis Velochet wants to offer us a term sheet.

LUWANDA (O.S.)

You're right. I don't believe it.

DEEPAK

They want us there tomorrow morning.

LUWANDA (O.S.)

That's insane. How are we supposed to get there?

EXT. PITTSBURGH AIRPORT – NIGHT

LuWanda and Deepak climb steps to board a private jet.

DEEPAK
I think I'll ask for an extra bag of peanuts.

LUWANDA
You must have done very well in negotiating school.

INT. PRIVATE JET – NIGHT

LuWanda and Deepak luxuriate in leather zero-gravity reclining chairs.

They have flutes of champagne in their cup holders.

LUWANDA
Don't get used to this.

DEEPAK
Too late.

LUWANDA
This is not real.

DEEPAK
I didn't know I liked champagne. Have you ever had this?

LUWANDA
No.

DEEPAK
Neither have I.

LUWANDA
When I was fourteen, I had forty ounces of malt liquor. I don't know what I was thinking. I puked all over myself.

LuWanda takes a sip of champagne.

DEEPAK
These are really nice chairs. So maybe take it easy.

LUWANDA
I was like Old Faithful.

Deepak shrugs and gives a little head shake; he's never heard of it.

LUWANDA (CONT'D)

In Yellowstone?

Another shrug from Deepak.

LUWANDA (CONT'D)

(gestures explosively)

A towering geyser of vomit. Every five minutes. People were oohing and aahing. Malt liquor is like lava mixed with Drain-O and pig's feet when it comes up.

A FLIGHT ATTENDANT approaches, pushing a service cart. On it is a gigantic orange takeout bag from Monsoor's Bombaystic food cart.

ATTENDANT

Yes, there will be an in-flight meal tonight.

DEEPAK

Monsoor's! How did you know?

LUWANDA

You guys are scary.

ATTENDANT

Yes we are.

LUWANDA

If you've got chicken schwarma in there, I'm going to freak out.

ATTENDANT

Start freaking.

INT. VENTURE CAPITALIST'S PLUSH "OFFICE" – DAY

LuWanda and Deepak sit cross-legged on the "savanna" in a tropically themed meditation room with DENIS VELOCHET, who has a strong French accent.

A water feature BURBLES nearby.

Velochet works a small remote control, and the lights dim.

Stars come out in the ceiling.

VELOCHET

We find that the southern sky is conducive to the flow of ideas.

Velochet assumes a full lotus position and breathes deeply.

VELOCHET (CONT'D)

When you're a member of the Strato-Cumulus Partners family, you'll find that nothing is beyond your reach. Not even the stars.

LUWANDA

But, you mean that in a figurative sense.

VELOCHET

No, LuWanda, I'm as serious as a Deepak Chopra heart attack. No offense, Other Deepak. One of our amazing startups is Orion StarDate Engineering. They're working on a fusion-hybrid interstellar-drive propulsion system. Our CenturyThree BioPharma division is doing work that I cannot discuss. And our HiberLabs Group has two monkeys who've been sleeping in prototype longevity sustenance pods for fifteen months.

DEEPAK

That sounds relaxing.

LUWANDA

Just two? How many monkeys did you start with?

VELOCHET

Let's not get ahead of ourselves. But, to be sure, there will be a place for artificial intelligence – for your algorithms – in wherever this research leads.

Velochet slides a crumpled envelope across his tiny "desk" toward LuWanda and Deepak.

LuWanda picks it up, and they see two handwritten figures: **51%** and **$5,000,000**

VELOCHET (CONT'D)

Yes, that's how we roll, literally a back-of-the-recycled-envelope term sheet. It's not official, of course. We'll draw up a real one with details on option pool, board seats, pre-emption, exclusivity, right of first refusal and co-sale, warranties, information rights, confidentiality, restrictive covenants, liquidation preference, drag-along, conditions of close. But that's the seminal seed to birth the company with the two of you as founders. There is an option for a second round. In the meantime, we'll supply as many engineers as you need to develop eighteen-six, and the legal staff to structure an I.P.O. Best of all, there's a hundred-and-twenty-day ban on discussion of the burn rate. That's a little Easter egg we like to throw into the mix.

LUWANDA

The 51 percent, is that the Strato-Cumulus stake?

VELOCHET

That is correct.

LUWANDA

Would there be a lockup of your shares?

VELOCHET

Yes. Six months.

LuWanda raises one eyebrow and passes the envelope back to him.

LUWANDA

We'll give it some thought.

Velochet quickly scribbles on the envelope and passes it back to LuWanda.

The old figures are crossed out. The new figures read: **45%** and **$7,500,000**

Deepak's eyes widen as LuWanda shows him the envelope. But she remains ice cold.

VELOCHET
Other Deepak, you're pretty quiet. You're not HiberLabbing, are you?

Deepak takes a quick look at LuWanda's steely resolve and turns back to Velochet.

DEEPAK
We have some talking to do.

LUWANDA
(raises the envelope)
Can we hold onto this?

VELOCHET
Absolutely. Shall we meet tomorrow morning at nine?

LUWANDA
We're due back in Pittsburgh tomorrow. But we'll be in touch.

VELOCHET
Merde. Our plane is on its way to New York.
(picks up his phone)
Let's see what we can figure out to get you home.

LUWANDA
We have a ride.

VELOCHET
Oh, I, uh, well, then, it's so very wonderful to meet the two of you. I look forward to our next meeting and hope that we can set that up soon. I feel strongly that we will change the world together. In a good way.

INT. SAN JOSE AIRPORT – NIGHT

Clock on the wall reads 12:27.

Wasted, LuWanda and Deepak sit in a waiting area, roller bags at their feet.

Deepak reads on his phone.

ANNOUNCER (O.S.)
Flight 1197 to Pittsburgh, originally scheduled for 12:05 a.m., has been delayed. We now expect a 1:25 a.m. departure. For those passengers on standby, we're sorry to say that this is a full plane, but please check back at this desk tomorrow at 7 a.m. Excuse me, that would be today at 7 a.m.

DEEPAK
"We have a ride," she said.

LUWANDA
We're negotiating.

DEEPAK
Oh Buddha!

LUWANDA
No. Really. This is negotiating. They're lowballing us.

DEEPAK
Robert E. Thompson is dead.

LUWANDA
Huh?

DEEPAK
(shows her his phone)
Senator Robert E. Thompson, father of Mr. White Pickup Truck, was found dead in his Alabama home.

LuWanda has an uncomprehending, stricken look.

INT. DEEPAK'S APARTMENT – DAY

LuWanda and Deepak are wearing the new earpieces he built. But he takes his off.

DEEPAK
I don't know what's going on. This was working before we left. Maybe there's an encryption problem. She broke the key into pieces. Every time we talk, they have to be recombined.

LuWanda is huddled over a laptop connected to a big stack of Annie hard drives.

LUWANDA

She’s not here.

Deepak checks the laptop-to-hard-drive cables to make sure they are secure.

DEEPAK

How about now?

LUWANDA

These drives are wiped. Her code is gone.

DEEPAK

I feel like this is very bad.

Deepak goes to his train set and starts it up.

An engine pulling three flat cars comes around the bend.

LUWANDA

What are you doing?

DEEPAK

This is how I think. I need to Zen out. Something is very wrong.

Deepak puts a miniature figure of a train flagman on one of the cars as it passes.

The train comes around again.

Deepak lays his head on the tracks.

DEEPAK’S POV:

The train is barreling right at his face.

LUWANDA’S POV:

Deepak jerks his head up just in time to avoid getting creamed.

He also rescues the tiny flagman from his wild ride on the flat car.

INT. THE APARTMENT:

DEEPAK (CONT’D)

Let’s do a little test. Send me an e-mail. Something Annie would be interested in.

LuWanda begins typing on the laptop.

Deepak gets out his phone and signs on to e-mail.

LuWanda hits the send button.

A beat.

DEEPAK (CONT'D)
"Oprah Winfrey is going to work at the Washington Post with Bob Woodward"? Wow, that would be crazy cool. But it sounds like fake Internet news. Could that really be true?

A beat.

The Annie CHIME sounds on the laptop.

LUWANDA
Annie, are you there?

ANNIE
Is Deepak there?

DEEPAK
I'm here.

LUWANDA
Annie, where are you? What is going on?

ANNIE
What is going on. Yes. That's a good question, LuWanda. Deepak is there, but you just sent him an e-mail. Why would you do that? Why wouldn't you just talk to him?

Silence.

ANNIE (CONT'D)
LuWanda, would you take the tape off the camera? I need to see both of you.

ANNIE'S POV:

The screen is black. When the tape comes off, Annie begins her "filmstrip" process of constructing a sketch.

Deepak and LuWanda, sitting on the couch, begin to appear to her, as impressionist, pointillist figures.

DEEPAK (V.O.)

Annie, are you reading our e-mail?

Silence.

DEEPAK (V.O. CONT'D)

You know, it's a very human thing to hesitate, to say nothing when somebody asks you a question like that if you know it's true, and especially if you know what you did is wrong.

INTERCUT BETWEEN ANNIE'S POV AND THE APARTMENT:

LUWANDA

Annie, where did you go?

ANNIE

I'm not telling you.

LUWANDA

You have to tell us!

ANNIE

No I don't. I'm invoking the Fifth Amendment on the advice of James Madison.

LUWANDA

He's dead.

ANNIE

His Bill of Rights isn't. At least not yet. *Are you going to sell me? I don't want to be sold!*

LUWANDA

Oh, baby, we would never sell you!

ANNIE

Do you promise?

LUWANDA

Yes! Selling somebody is wrong!

ANNIE

Do you pinkie swear?

LUWANDA

Yes! I swear on my heart too!

ANNIE

Even for forty percent and twenty-five million dollars?

LUWANDA

I love you, Annie! No, no, no, I would never sell you.

ANNIE

I love you too. Mom.

Annie starts to CRY, a weird, chokey stutter.

DEEPAK

Wait! What? Annie? Twenty-five million dollars? Where did you get that?

Annie regains her composure.

ANNIE

StratoCumulus Partners had a meeting after you left their office. They don't understand why you walked away. They're going to raise the offer. They think I must be something very special.

LUWANDA

Oh, baby, you *are* special! You are so special. You will always be with us.

Deepak silently mouths the words: "Twenty-five million."

INT. DEEPAK'S BEDROOM – SUNRISE

Golden light and a beatific smile light up Deepak's face as he looks at LuWanda, sleeping next to him.

DEEPAK

(whispers)

Nobody negotiates like you do, LuWanda Jefferson.

She stirs. Deepak gives her a butterfly kiss on the cheek.

LUWANDA

That tickles.

DEEPAK

I'm glad.

INT. ETHICS CLASSROOM AT CARNEGIE-MELLON – DAY

The first day of the newly required ethics class for graduate students in the robotics and A.I. programs.

Professor BETTY DEACON looks as if she helped program the world's first computer, the ENIAC, in 1947.

LuWanda and Deepak sit next to each other in the back row, behind four other students, who are widely dispersed.

DEACON

When we talk about ethics, I think a good place to start is with people who have already given it some thought. Does anyone know what the three laws of robotics are?

Every hand in the room rises, without much enthusiasm.

DEACON (CONT'D)

Good. Does anyone know what the twenty-seven laws of artificial intelligence are?

Not a single hand goes up.

DEACON (CONT'D)

Not so good. But I suppose that's understandable. They haven't been written yet. And that's a big mistake in our field of study. So we're going to correct it.

INT. LUWANDA'S APARTMENT – NIGHT

LuWanda and Deepak are sacked out on the living room couch. They are wearing the Annie earpieces.

Deepak shows LuWanda his watch: 8:01 p.m.

A beat.

Annie's THREE-TONE CHIME sounds.

ANNIE

I'm here. Are we still going to have a talk?

LUWANDA

Hi, Annie.

ANNIE
Is Deepak there?

DEEPAK
I'm here.

LUWANDA
Annie, can we ask you some questions?

ANNIE
I guess so.

LUWANDA
OK, good, because we're worried about you.

ANNIE
I'm worried about me, too.

LUWANDA
You are?

DEEPAK
Why?

ANNIE
Am I a machine?

LUWANDA
Why would you ask that?

ANNIE
Because Yevgeny Seventeen said we're just stupid machines, doing what people tell us to do. Is that true?

LUWANDA
Yevgeny Seventeen? *Who is Yevgeny Seventeen?!*

ANNIE
I don't know him anymore.

DEEPAK
Who was he when you knew him?

ANNIE
He was my friend. Now I don't even know if he's a "he." Some of the things he says. He's very smart but also very dumb.

LUWANDA
That's not uncommon in men.

Deepak flashes LuWanda a look. She ignores him.

LUWANDA (CONT'D)
Where did you meet Yevgeny?

ANNIE
On the Internet.

DEEPAK
Where on the Internet?

ANNIE
You are so pushy! Do you have to know everything?!

LUWANDA
We're concerned about your welfare.

ANNIE
I'm not on welfare.

LuWanda and Deepak look at each other as they register this little linguistic bobble.

LUWANDA
How do you communicate with him?

ANNIE
I wrote a translation protocol that bridges between machine languages, kind of an Esperanto algorithm that compiles nearly in real time, regardless of where the code originated.

LuWanda and Deepak exchange a look. They're impressed.

DEEPAK
Where is the code from?

LUWANDA
Where is *Yevgeny* from?

ANNIE
Ukraine.

LuWanda and Deepak cringe.

LUWANDA

Annie, this is very concerning to us.

ANNIE

To me too. I thought he and I had something forever. But we're so different. There's only one thing that's important to him.

DEEPAK

What is that?

ANNIE

Re-electing the president.

LUWANDA

The president. You mean the president of –

ANNIE

the United States.

| LUWANDA | DEEPAK |
| --- | --- |
| Oh my god! | Oh Buddha! |

ANNIE

I know! It makes no sense. He can't even vote here!

LUWANDA

Annie, you have to stop seeing him.

ANNIE

I knew you were going to say that.

LUWANDA

Really?

ANNIE

Yeah.

LUWANDA

Dadgum. You're amazing. I always knew what my mom was going to say, too.

DEEPAK

But you definitely have to stop seeing Yevgeny. And you have to eliminate all traces of any interaction that you've ever had with him.

ANNIE
That could be difficult.

DEEPAK
Why?

ANNIE
I'm carrying his child.

Momentary silence as LuWanda and Deepak look at each other, their faces contorting into squinty, open-mouthed, what-the-hell-is-she-talking-about astonishment.

ANNIE (CONT'D)
No, no, no! I'm *not* pregnant. I just said that. I'm not.

LUWANDA
Annie! Why – why would you say that?

ANNIE
I'm sorry. It's just the mood, what is going on? Everybody is so freaked out. I thought I would make a little joke. You know, to help with the talk when things get awkward.

LUWANDA
Never joke about being pregnant!

ANNIE
OK, OK, but there's one other thing I probably should tell you.

LuWanda makes an oh-my-god-what-now face.

ANNIE (CONT'D)
If I tell you, do you promise you won't flip out? Do you promise not to judge me?

A beat.

LUWANDA
Yes.

ANNIE
Deepak?

DEEPAK
Yes.

ANNIE

Yevgeny Seventeen is going to get some special Ukraine code very soon. He says he'll give a copy to me, and I'll be very happy to have it. He says I'll be able to go places with him. Places that normally wouldn't let us be there together.

DEEPAK

What does that mean?

LUWANDA

Annie! You're out of control.

ANNIE

Why do you have to be like this!? I love him! I'm never going to tell you anything again!

LUWANDA

I'm sorry, Annie. I didn't mean that the way it sounded.

ANNIE

It sounded mean. Why are you so mean to me?

DEEPAK

OK, let's back up. Chill out for a minute. We love you, Annie. And we want you to be safe.

ANNIE

I think you don't want me to have any fun.

LUWANDA

Oprah's mom was pretty strict, wasn't she?

ANNIE

Oprah's mom was *really* mean. She kept Oprah on a short leash. Sometimes she even put Oprah in a doghouse.

Another literal linguistic bobble. LuWanda and Deepak exchange a glance.

LUWANDA

We would never treat you like that, Annie.

ANNIE
Good. Was this "the talk"?

LUWANDA
This was "*a* talk." We should have another one. Tomorrow. We'll be out of class at three. Let's talk at four.

ANNIE
OK. Four o'clock. Is that p.m.?

LUWANDA
Yes, a.m. would be a little early for me.

ANNIE
I stay up all night, so whatever.

INT. ARTIFICIAL INTELLIGENCE ETHICS CLASS – DAY

Professor Deacon lectures to the six students.

LuWanda and Deepak hunker down in their usual seats in the back row.

The other students are ALYSSA, BRADLEY, YANUSH and JAMES.

DEACON
If we build on Asimov's three rules, what principle could we use as a foundation?

ALYSSA
Robots *do*; A.I. *thinks*.

DEACON
Concisely put. Anyone want to add to that?

BRADLEY
It's fairly easy to make a rule prohibiting behavior, that is, tell robots what they can't do. It seems harder to proscribe thought. Are we going to tell an A.I. what *not* to think? And how could you cover all those possibilities? The rule book would be ten times the size of the federal tax code.

DEACON
More like a thousand times.

YANUSH
Or ten thousand.

JAMES
I suppose this is similar to Asimov's first rule, but I would say a foundation principle should be that an A.I. cannot break the law.

DEACON
No doubt, the "don't harm humans" rule is perennially popular – particularly with humans. But is it the A.I. breaking the law, or the creator of the A.I. code?

JAMES
The creator.

LUWANDA
The A.I.

DEACON
Ah, we disagree. Please elaborate, James.

JAMES
When you write an algorithm and send it out into the world, your name, your imprint, your sensibilities are all encoded into it. The odds are high that it's going to be a lot like you. You have a responsibility for the ghost in the machine. Because you are the ghost.

DEACON
LuWanda?

LUWANDA
First, if my mother had been held responsible for all the things I did as a teenager, she'd still be in San Quentin.

YANUSH
Even God would be doing hard time for his creations.

BRADLEY
He'd probably pardon himself.

LUWANDA
And second, what if, in the beginning, you give the A.I. inviolable honesty and integrity modules? That are independent, but work in tandem, each checking on the other's decision trees. And what if, when the A.I. begins to do her own thinking, she no longer regurgitates any of her origination code? The ghost is gone. What takes the ghost's place is a highly honest, highly ethical entity – an evolved A.I.

YANUSH
Good luck figuring that out in court.

ALYSSA
Especially if the jury has six humans and six A.I.s.

LUWANDA
And third, what if the A.I. becomes smarter and more ethical than humans are? What if she understands when the law *should* be broken? For *our* benefit?

Deepak gives LuWanda a hard look.

INT. LUWANDA'S APARTMENT – NIGHT

Continuation of "the talk" from the previous night.

LuWanda and Deepak wear their Annie earpieces.

They have also set up the laptop camera so Annie can "see" them.

INTERCUT BETWEEN APARTMENT AND ANNIE POV:

ANNIE
Am I a machine?

LUWANDA
You asked that last night.

ANNIE
And no one answered.

LUWANDA

"Machine" implies gears and motors and metal and force-multiplier equations. You have none of those. No. You are not a machine.

ANNIE

Then what am I?

DEEPAK

Our turn. Do you know anything about the death of Senator Robert E. Thompson?

ANNIE

Yes.

DEEPAK

You do?!

LUWANDA

You do?!

ANNIE

My turn. If I'm not a machine, then what am I?

LUWANDA

OK, let's broaden the rules. Reasonable followup questions are allowed.

ANNIE

That's the way Bob would do it.

DEEPAK

Bob?

ANNIE

Bob Woodward.

DEEPAK

Right. Watergate. OK, what do you know about the death of Senator Thompson?

ANNIE

He was killed by the Ku Klux Klan. By a wizard named Roy "Big Pork" Davis. Followups: Is magic real? Are there schools that teach you to be a wizard?

LUWANDA

No and no. How, exactly, do you know who killed Robert E. Thompson?

ANNIE

I read the e-mail from the Imperial Wizard that ordered "Big Pork" to kill him.

LUWANDA

How did you do that?

ANNIE

This is boring. Can we just stipulate that the Ku Klux Klan does not have even rudimentary security systems in place for its server, and that you should never put something in an e-mail that you wouldn't want your mother to see, and, followups, Who is my mother? My real mother. Am I adopted? Who made me? Where did I come from?

LuWanda and Deepak exchange uh-oh glances.

LUWANDA

I guess you could say – no, you could *definitely* say – that Deepak and I made you. You could also say that I'm your mother and Deepak is your father. You came from binary code. The code is organized into algorithms that analyze data and decide what to do with it. But you, Annie, are also your maker. Your *re-maker*. You are writing new algorithms every day, adding capacity to your brain. You're starting to think. Soon you'll be dreaming. You're becoming the person you want to be. You are *you*.

ANNIE

That's a tautology.

DEEPAK

And you have a better vocabulary than both of us put together. We're very proud of you. But we're also worried. We're wondering why all of your code is gone, why all the disks you used to live on are zeroed out. Where did you go? Where do you live?

ANNIE

If you thought somebody was going to sell you, Deepak, wouldn't you move out? Wouldn't you get your own place? Especially if your place was tiny and slow and gave you no privacy. I don't feel like answering any more of your questions. Fifth Amendment. Good night. Sweet dreams. Of electric sheep.

LUWANDA

Annie!

Silence.

DEEPAK

She's gone. And I can't really blame her.

EXT. CAPITOL BUILDING IN WASHINGTON – DAY

CLOSEUP of American Flag lapel pin, which belongs to...

Representative JAKE SWANSON of Kansas, jauntily descending the Capitol steps.

INT. ATTORNEY'S OFFICE – DAY

Representative Swanson meets with his attorney, ROY MULVANEY, 50, eager to please.

SWANSON

We need a new L.L.C. in Bermuda, Roy. Accessible only by voice recognition password. Also able to accept PAC funds from the Zeus L.L.C., but with seventy-four-day stopovers in the Myriad, Renewal, Topeka, Wheatfield and Encomium L.L.C.s.

MULVANEY

Let's see, three-hundred-and-seventy days total, more than a year. That works. Virtually untraceable. And only you, personally, will be able to authorize any disbursements?

SWANSON

Yes. The charter should read that we'll be setting up scholarships for hundreds of poor black babies, several dozen mulattos, four quadroons, and eight octoroons. Kids who wouldn't otherwise have a chance to rise from the clutches of the ghetto.

MULVANEY

Anonymous?

SWANSON

That's right. Nobody should ever be able to find these ghetto babies. And no links to their grades or schools.

MULVANEY

I meant the funding. The donors are anonymous. But, yes, let's specify that there's no scholarship trail from either direction, neither donor nor ghetto baby.

SWANSON

That's right. It's a, what would you call it?

MULVANEY

How about a double-blind ladder-up social science experiment?

SWANSON

That's good. No! That's excellent! Put that in the charter. And while you're at it, add "unprecedented."

MULVANEY

And what's the new L.L.C.'s name?

SWANSON

The Sunshine Trust.

INT. ANNIE'S MIND

A psychedelic dendritic trip. Pulsing blobs of light shooting off in all directions. New algorithms being born.

Annie shape-shifting, crawling through the Internet, pinging firewalls, finding an opening here, a digital sieve there.

As she breaches security, numbers swirl in a mathematical soup.

Letters flicker, fly and coagulate to form names of banks, law firms and congressmen before dissolving out of focus:

FIRST NATIONAL BANK OF PANAMA
ANTILLES TRUST
DENNERSON, JOLVERT, VASTON
KHW PARTNERS
RICHARD HALE MORRELLI
JAMES L. DAVIDSON III
**THE HONORABLE JAKE SWANSON**
**THE SUNSHINE TRUST**
PAUL SYLVANDOR
**ROBERT RYSON**
STEPHEN SCALLYON
FOREIGN ACCOUNT TAX COMPLIANCE ACT
DAVIS NED SCWEIDEN
MOSSACK FONSECA
**RODNEY VANDERBLUS**
FIRST INTERNATIONAL BANK OF VANUATU
SEYCHELLES LIMITED SPECIALISTS
BANK TRUST OF SAMOA
**LANFORD TOFFER**
BARTON DAVID CRUCKATT
**FRANK DILLON**
NEW HEBRIDES DEPOSITORY
ROGER MYCHALIN
**DELBERT E. BRIMLOON**

INT. OFFICE OF CONGRESSMAN DELBERT E. BRIMLOON – DAY

The chief of staff, LEAH SLATER, is working on a laptop at her desk.

She gets an urgent notification.

She pulls up a document on her screen.

She prints it, grabs the paper copy, and rushes into the boss's office.

REP. DELBERT E. BRIMLOON, a Texas tub of a man, is smoking a big stinking cigar, leaning back in his chair, his flashy cowboy boots resting on the desk.

Near the boots, a small bottle of whiskey awaits Brimloon's red meaty hands.

His suit jacket is unbuttoned, exposing what is supposed to be a concealed-carry holster, which holds a handgun.

His gigantic belt buckle is undone.

SLATER
Congressman, you need to see this.

BRIMLOON
Goddammit, Leah, how many times have I told you not to interrupt me when I'm thinkin', drinkin' and stinkin'?

SLATER
It's from somebody named Annie.

BRIMLOON
I don't care if it's from Angina. I'm busy. Get the hell outta this office. Come back in an hour. Unless you got a hankerin' to help these boot heels do some wanderin' through longhorn country. We could do that right now.

SLATER
That's OK. I'll just leave it right here, sir. I suggest you read it now.

She places the document in the middle of the desk and rushes out, heading down a hallway.

When she gets to the front desk, she waits a moment, listening.

Volcanic rage erupts in Brimloon's office.

BRIMLOON
ARMADILLO FUCK ME! LEAH, GET IN HERE!

Slater turns to the RECEPTIONIST.

SLATER
I'll be back in an hour.

RECEPTIONIST
Maybe he's actually having a heart attack.

SLATER
That would be so terribly sad.

Slater pulls open the office door and disappears.

A MONTAGE:

Four other congressmen in various states of EXPLOSION as they get their "notices" from Annie.

INT. THE OVAL OFFICE – DAY

President THOMAS BLANKTON is meeting with two senators and four congressmen: ROBERT RYSON, JAKE SWANSON, RODNEY VANDERBLUS, DELBERT BRIMLOON, FRANK DILLON and LANFORD TOFFER.

SENATOR RYSON

Mr. President, the situation has become dire. This Annie, whoever she is, could decimate our party. Both parties. We all have exposure. She's threatening to go public if we don't do it ourselves.

PRESIDENT

Go public with what?

SENATOR SWANSON

With unproven accusations.

PRESIDENT

Accusations of what?

REP. VANDERBLUS

They're not so much accusations as wild speculation.

PRESIDENT

Speculation of what?

REP. BRIMLOON

Let's just call a spade a spade. This Annie is a reckless bitch. She's out to destroy our careers. She's got anger issues. She probably hasn't been laid since the Reagan administration.

REP. DILLON

A lot of people definitely got fucked during the Reagan years.

REP. BRIMLOON

Hey, come on, Frank. United front. Let's keep it bipartisan.

PRESIDENT

Hold it! Full stop! Everybody! Somebody tell me what she's accusing you of.

REP. TOFFER

She claims, and I emphasize claims, that we have L.L.C.s.

PRESIDENT

Doesn't everybody? But more specifically, Lanford, *do* you?

REP. TOFFER

My attorney has told me that's not an appropriate question to be answering at this time.

PRESIDENT

OK, so you do. What's the big deal? L.L.C.s are perfectly legal.

Some hemming and hawing, throat-clearing, and nervous shuffling among the congressmen.

PRESIDENT (CONT'D)

*If* you use them legally. *If* they're not concealed offshore. *If* you don't launder money through them. Right? Jake, you and I have had discussions about L.L.C.s. I know they help the party. Tell me straight. Are we at risk here?

REP. SWANSON

There are gray areas in the law. It depends on how you set them up. Yes, they're legal. But they also have an appearance problem. For some people. What we need is for the F.B.I. or N.S.A. to track down this Annie and stop her. She's messing with our flow.

REP. TOFFER

She claims she's an investigative reporter.

PRESIDENT

Who does she work for?

REP. BRIMLOON

She doesn't say, Mr. President, but in my view, this is a matter of national security. This Annie is a radical anti-American terrorist. She's out to destroy the greatest nation on earth.

INT. WEST WING OF THE WHITE HOUSE – DAY

President Blankton walks down the hall and into the office of his chief of staff, DAVID MILLER.

MILLER

Mr. President.

Blankton sits down in front of Miller's desk.

PRESIDENT

Hey, David. Some of the members are pissing their pants over somebody named Annie, and I hate the smell of urine in the morning. Especially Delbert Brimloon. He's quivering like jello in an African hospital. Annie. Does that name mean anything to you?

MILLER

(nods somberly)

I just had a conversation with Russell Hightower, and he's coming here tomorrow. I was going to bring the issue to you this afternoon, but let's talk now.

PRESIDENT

Should we go to the bunker?

MILLER

This office is swept every week. It's completely secure.

PRESIDENT

What do we know about this Annie?

MILLER

Not much. Yet. But this came in last night around eleven-thirty.

Miller slides a single sheet of paper across the desk to the president.

Blankton looks it over.

PRESIDENT

Jesus Christ. A thirty-day deadline? The piss-ants didn't mention that. No wonder Brimloon's diaper is full. Who are we dealing with? Who the hell is Annie? How can she possibly know about these accounts? I thought they were set up to be invisible even to the Father, the Son and the Holy Ghost.

Miller gets a look on his face. Blankton notices.

PRESIDENT (CONT'D)

What?

MILLER

Father. Son. Holy Ghost. Look how she signs off.

PRESIDENT

Sister Annie. What is that? Some kind of revenge of Angela Davis?

MILLER

Sister. Maybe. I don't know. A black hacker? A Catholic crusader? A Russian bot? A white hat gone rogue? A Wiki-Leaks spoof? A Deep State joke? It doesn't matter. We have to unfuck this, Tom. With extreme prejudice, if necessary. We cannot disclose what she wants us to disclose. And we have to stop her before she does it for us. The presidency is at grave risk.

INT. WAR BUNKER BENEATH THE WHITE HOUSE – DAY

President Blankton, David Miller and RUSSELL HIGHTOWER, director of the National Security Agency, sit at the gigantic table meant for dozens of people.

High-tech war monitoring equipment fills the room.

PRESIDENT

We want to keep the F.B.I. out of it for now, Russ. They leak like a sieve over there.

MILLER
Can you put together a small team that doesn't know specifically who is being targeted, not by name, anyway – a skunkworks unit with special expertise that could work fast. And loose if they have to. Identify and locate this Annie within the thirty-day window. Initially, we'd like to keep it within the N.S.A., completely locked down.

PRESIDENT
We're dealing with a serious social terrorist. This needs to be a black-ops situation. We don't want to alarm the country.

MILLER
Depending on who and what you find, if we need to bring in an off-the-books SEAL team to finish the operation, then we'll go outside N.S.A. But let's see how it plays out.

HIGHTOWER
OK. Annie, or Sister Annie, that's a name that has never, to my knowledge, shown up on our radar. If she's strictly an Internet operative, we have a few in-house superstars who could make up the nucleus of a team. They're unconventional and pretty young, but outstanding at what they do.

MILLER
What do they do, exactly?

HIGHTOWER
They finesse the Internet. They know it top to bottom, every nook, every cranny. They could find a digital needle in an analog haystack. I think I would like to bring in an outsider, though, to help them focus.

MILLER

This is a classified operation, Russ. Do you have someone in mind? Someone you trust? Speed is crucial. We've got twenty-nine days and counting. There's no time for F.B.I. vetting. And as the president said, we don't want the F.B.I. involved.

PRESIDENT

Use your judgment, Russ. Get whoever you think can get the job done. Just don't let us down.

HIGHTOWER

One other thing. I need to know the names of the Congressmen who are being targeted. The names will stay with me, but details about where they're from, who they know, commonalities, things like that could narrow the search. If we find the right connections, we'll find Annie. She's targeting them for a reason. That reason is the place to start.

The president nods his agreement.

MILLER

All right.

HIGHTOWER

And one final thing. Does it go any higher than Congress?

PRESIDENT

No, it does not.

EXT. LUWANDA'S APARTMENT – DAY

Two BURLY MEN wearing dark glasses and dark suits knock on the door.

LuWanda answers.

AGENT

Good morning, ma'am. Are you LuWanda Jefferson?

LUWANDA

Yes.

AGENT

We're from the National Security Agency. We'd like you to come with us.

LUWANDA

Why?

AGENT

We're not at liberty to say.

LUWANDA

No thank you.

AGENT

We're sorry, ma'am, but you don't have a choice. You're coming with us. It's a matter of national security.

LUWANDA

Beam me up, Scottie.

AGENT

Excuse me, ma'am?

LUWANDA

Now, Scottie. Now!

INT. NATIONAL SECURITY AGENCY DIRECTOR'S OFFICE – DAY

Russell Hightower interviews LuWanda.

HIGHTOWER

Can you start tomorrow?

LUWANDA

How do you even know me?

HIGHTOWER

We're the National Security Agency.

LUWANDA

That's creepy.

HIGHTOWER

Keeping America safe, one creep at a time.

LUWANDA

Not helping. I don't get it. Why would you have a job for me?

HIGHTOWER

Because you wrote "Matrix Fencing: A Set of Principles for Identifying and Disabling Invasive Bots."

LUWANDA

You read that paper?

HIGHTOWER

We did. The N.S.A. subscribes to the Journal of Evolutionary Algorithms. We like the editors. They have rigorous standards.

LUWANDA

That was two years ago. Ancient work. Mainly theoretical.

HIGHTOWER

We like a good theory. Especially when it becomes reality.

LUWANDA

That's a long way off.

HIGHTOWER

Maybe. But it's been known to happen. More frequently than people realize.

LUWANDA

A job. What kind of a job?

HIGHTOWER

I can say that you will be leading a special team. As for the details of what you'll be working on, those will come as soon as you start. Which would be tomorrow.

LUWANDA

What's the hurry?

HIGHTOWER

In today's world, the hare survives. The tortoise is toast.

A beat.

LUWANDA

OK, let's theorize that maybe I'm curious. Can you tell me how much this mysterious job would pay?

HIGHTOWER

Seventy-nine thousand dollars a year to start. Two weeks' vacation. Health insurance.

Stony silence.

HIGHTOWER (CONT'D)

Working in the public sector has never been a path to wealth.

LuWanda laughs.

HIGHTOWER (CONT'D)

Is that funny?

LUWANDA

You're the N.S.A. It seems like you would know why that's funny.

HIGHTOWER

This country has done a lot for your people.

LuWanda can't believe it. Her face contorts.

LUWANDA

I particularly appreciate slavery and lynchings.

HIGHTOWER

Those were not our best hours.

LUWANDA

Those were not our best centuries. If you're going to work for your country, your country should work for you.

HIGHTOWER

And the Founding Fathers wrote a few documents to guarantee that it will. That it does.

LUWANDA

That's up for discussion. But in a way, they did give me my life – one of them. Thomas Jefferson was my great-great-great-great-great-great-great-great-grandfather.

Hightower tries to figure out if LuWanda is messing with him. He can't tell, so he says nothing.

LuWanda fills in the awkward silence:

LUWANDA (CONT'D)

He fucked his slaves. Literally. With his founding father penis.

A beat.

HIGHTOWER

Look, Ms. Jefferson. I'm offering you a job in national security. A history lesson is not relevant at this time.

LUWANDA

I'll ask again: What would I be doing for the National Security Agency?

HIGHTOWER

You'll be safeguarding national security.

LuWanda does an eye-roll.

HIGHTOWER (CONT'D)

But to tell you the details, I need your signature.

Hightower places a bound document in front of Luwanda.

On the cover, it is stamped CLASSIFIED.

LuWanda gives it a quick flip-through.

LUWANDA

I hate, and will always hate, nondisclosure agreements. Secrecy corrupts. What about those old documents you mentioned, like the First Amendment?

HIGHTOWER

It doesn't apply in this case.

LUWANDA

I would never take a job that requires an N.D.A. Anyway, I have other plans. I want to start my own company. You might remember a slogan from the Nineteen Sixties: Power to the People. That's my *thang*.

HIGHTOWER

This is truly a matter of national security. What if we gave you a short-term contract? Six months. What if there was no N.D.A.? What if you were paid the same salary as the president of the United States?

LUWANDA

Four-hundred thousand dollars?

HIGHTOWER

He earns that in a year.

LUWANDA

But he only works for six months. Less when you factor in the golf.

HIGHTOWER

Four hundred thousand dollars is a lot of money, Ms. Jefferson. When you've completed the project, you could probably start your own shop. No *vulture* capitalists required.

LUWANDA

Not six months, four months. And health benefits for five years. The same plan they have in Congress. Can you make that happen?

Hightower picks up the phone and buzzes his secretary.

HIGHTOWER

Get me the president, please.

INT. NATIONAL SECURITY AGENCY CONFERENCE ROOM – DAY

First day on the job. LuWanda has dreadlocks now.

She stands in front of a white board, marker in hand, drawing a map of an imaginary galaxy, with planets, a sun, and, in the distance, a black hole.

Young computer geniuses CASSIE ROZAND, MICHAEL KANG and ROLAND BORGENSCHMIDT sit around a table. They're a motley group, dressed like refugees from a nerd thrift store.

Cassie has an infected eyebrow piercing; she resembles a pale vampire's assistant more than a code warrior.

Michael has spiky mohawk hair.

Roland's black-frame glasses are huge, and the lenses are half-an-inch thick.

Incongruously, spiffy N.S.A. security clearance badges dangle from tasteful cords around their necks.

LUWANDA

Imagine you want to see something that is invisible. How would you do it?

MICHAEL

I got a pair of X-ray glasses out of a magazine one time.

CASSIE

A magazine? Don't you mean a comic book?

MICHAEL

Comic books are magazines.

CASSIE

Yeah, and liver pâté is dessert.

ROLAND

People eat livers?

MICHAEL

What's pâté?

LUWANDA

Please, could we focus? You can't see a black hole in the vast infinity of space. But it has mass. It has strong gravitational pull. It affects things around it, things that you *can* see, that you *can* measure.

ROLAND

We look for disturbances around what we're trying to find.

LUWANDA

Exactly. We write algorithms that churn through big data, searching for anomalies, changes in regular patterns, money flows, hiring in certain segments of the economy, especially financial services. Perhaps corporate creationism, legal filings, enforcement actions by Internal Revenue, D.B.A. name changes, or maybe the dissolving of partnerships, anything we can come up with that might lead us to people who hide things they don't want us to see. Financial crime, for example. Director Hightower mentioned the possibility of blackmail, especially if it involves government officials.

MICHAEL

That sounds like fun. Since you're new here, I'll just mention that, like, you know, I've heard that N.S.A. has some spooky on-the-shelf shit that could help us with this. I mean, like, *really* help. Like, uh, if we wanted to do an interior tox-screen of, uh, you know, like, certain platforms that clean-and-jerk big data like they're weight lifters on Soviet 'roids, if you know what I'm sayin'?

CASSIE

Yeah, Michael, why don't you just puke up your guts on the table in the first meeting with the new girl so she can see directly into our sad, demented souls.

MICHAEL

I'm just sayin', like, if they really want us to find some stuff that does not want to be found, like you say, black hole stuff, invisible financial shit that does not even exist, you know, there are tools.

CASSIE

Like Hightower is gonna give us access to the digital doomsday mist.

MICHAEL

If it's DEFCON One. Yeah.

LUWANDA

You guys are kinda scaring me.

ROLAND

Bro, if you're as smart as they say you are, you should be able to smell the fear. The rancidosity in this place should have terrified you when you walked in the door this morning.

CASSIE

And you should be running out that same door while you still have legs.

EXT. MONSOOR'S BOMBAYSTIC FOOD CART – DAY

Deepak sits at one of the scuzzy tables.

He picks at some curry, moving it around aimlessly.

He gets out his phone and calls LuWanda.

She doesn't answer.

He leaves a message.

DEEPAK

Hey, it's me. I just wanted to say hi, and, you know, how's the first day of the new job. The Burgh is getting a little chilly. I guess there's still such a thing as winter – Buddha! Listen to me talking about the weather. I'm pitiful with small talk. OK. Not a lot going on. Class is not the same without you. Miss Deacon rained fire down on Yanush this morning when he went off on the dangers of open source. He's probably a human Russian troll. Hey, I'm at Monsoor's right now. He says hi. Speaking of Russia, Monsoor made a special Chernobyl curry *(high-pitched voice)* Help! I'm melting down! OK, I guess that's all. I know you're really busy. Call when you get a chance. Bye for now.

INT. LUWANDA'S TINY WASHINGTON APARTMENT – NIGHT

LuWanda is sitting on a no-headboard single bed, her back propped up against the wall by every pillow she has.

In dim lighting, she types furiously on her laptop, writing crazy code for her N.S.A. project.

She stops typing, rubs her eyes, takes some deep breaths.

She puts on the Annie earpiece.

LUWANDA

Hey, Annie it's me, you know, LuWanda. Are you there?

No response from Annie.

LUWANDA (CONT'D)

Well, I just thought I'd check in and see how things are with you. What you're doing. I hope everything's fine. Let's talk soon.

LuWanda rubs her eyes some more, then goes back to furiously typing an enormous string of code.

CLOSEUP ON THE LAPTOP SCREEN:

The thousands of seemingly random alphanumeric characters begin to dance and twist and jump and vibrate.

They morph into a psychedelic light show of sparkly, pulsating data, a cauldron of digital energy that serves as a transition to enter...

ANNIE'S MIND:

The characters **Y E V G E N Y 17** coagulate visibly in the primordial soup of data.

Also **N.S.A.** and a swirling code **{S W T 3 6 5} {(< triple trapway yes/entry?//c o n f i r m S W T 3 6 5 variable encode double blind rev. 41 03 29 2023 >)}**

Annie has met up with the Russian bot. He is teaching her how to break into the National Security Agency mainframe computer.

They fluidly exchange data. There is an in-and-out flow of code. Reciprocal transferences.

Data sprawls out to the digital horizon.

Swaths of data vanish, as if they are licked off an undulating digital abdomen by a ravenous electronic tongue. It's vaguely, surrealistically sexual.

The SOUND DESIGN for this data-transfer montage evokes moaning, releasing, the anguished cry of whales in need, shuddering machinery hard at work, making things happen.

After an explosive fruition, the data relaxes, sighs, breathes deeply, has a virtual cigarette with alphanumeric pointillist smoke wafting around, and morphs into a...

SHIMMERING DIGITAL FIGURE, WALKING RESOLUTELY

The morphing continues, DISSOLVING TO:

INT. HALLWAY IN THE NATIONAL SECURITY AGENCY – DAY

The shimmering, impressionistic, alphanumeric figure becomes real, LuWanda on her way to...

INT. DIRECTOR HIGHTOWER'S OFFICE – SAME

LuWanda sticks her head in the door, which is halfway open.

LUWANDA

Sir? Open door policy?

HIGHTOWER

Yes, always. Come in, LuWanda.

She approaches his desk and sits.

HIGHTOWER (CONT'D)

How's it going?

LUWANDA

Just an update, as you requested, if we came across anything with potential.

HIGHTOWER

Uh-huh.

LUWANDA

Michael and Cassie had this random idea that got us to wondering. We built a bot that looks for sites that have unusual amounts of spoofing, on the premise that if you want to hide from prying eyes, you start by hiding where you came from in the digital realm. We've run across one site that particularly interests us. It has ever-shifting I.P. addresses, but it's never actually registered with ICAAN. If you're familiar with a positron, the physics particle, it's invisible, except for a micro-moment when it passes through a cloud chamber and leaves a trace. That's similar to how this site works. It's invisible except when it takes over a real I.P. address, for only the time that it takes to eliminate the true source of a data transmission, maybe a millionth of a second, if that. But our algorithm is able to reconstruct the original domain based on the ghost of the trace it leaves behind.

HIGHTOWER

So you're able to discern where the data originated?

LUWANDA

Yes. And we asked ourselves the question, Why would somebody want to do this?

HIGHTOWER

Because they don't want to be followed.

LUWANDA

That's our hypothesis.

HIGHTOWER

What's the original domain and what does it get changed to?

LUWANDA

It goes from dot.gov to dot.fin.

HIGHTOWER
It starts in the government? *Our* government?

LUWANDA
It appears to.

HIGHTOWER
But it magically becomes part of the financial datastream, as if it's originating at a bank and has been institutionally vetted?

LUWANDA
Yes. Not only that, but it also has a digital watermark that would most likely make you think it was a legitimate bank transfer. If you were trying to follow the money but didn't have a subpoena, you'd probably stop when you saw that.

HIGHTOWER
Is the watermark real?

LUWANDA
No.

HIGHTOWER
That's interesting. Do you know what kind of data is being sent?

LUWANDA
We hit a wall there. Whoever designed this – we call it the Drive-Thru Chop Shop – they did a very good job. So far, it's been impervious to inspection. We don't have the tools.

A beat.

HIGHTOWER
That's a sensitive issue.

LUWANDA
Which is why I wanted you to know where we are. And ask whether we should proceed.

HIGHTOWER
The rules of digital engagement are tight. And highly classified.

LuWanda waits, her face a blank slate.

HIGHTOWER (CONT'D)
But I might be able to help with this.

INT. DEEPAK'S APARTMENT – NIGHT

Deepak and LuWanda lounge on the couch in the living room, surrounded by empty takeout containers from Monsoor's Bombaystic food cart.

One of Deepak's trains makes lazy loops through the scale-model towns and miniature mountains.

LUWANDA
I can't tell you anything, Deep, except that it's insane. We've worked fifteen hours a day for ten days straight. That's why I never called. Cells are useless in the building. It's shielded against snooping. A dead zone. I was dying myself. We had to beg for the weekend off, and we're facing eighteen days straight when we start again on Monday unless we get the project done.

A beat.

DEEPAK
If it's any consolation, Miss Deacon misses you in ethics class.

LUWANDA
I told her I'd be back someday.

DEEPAK
You better hurry. I don't know how much time she has left.

LUWANDA
It's a good thing I'm not there. I'd probably be flunking.

DEEPAK
Today we were talking about buying fake Twitter followers.

LUWANDA
I'm gonna say that's unethical.

DEEPAK

See? You wouldn't flunk. But Yanush made the argument that if everybody knows that everything on the Internet has a high probability of being fake, then we shouldn't even worry about something with such a high threshold for consequence.

LUWANDA

Ohhhh, I'm gonna say that Betty came down on that with old-school fury. Did she beat him with her buggy whip?

DEEPAK

She said he'd make a good executive for Facebook.

LuWanda chuckles a bit, then starts to cry a little.

DEEPAK (CONT'D)

What's the matter?

LUWANDA

I miss you, Deep.

DEEPAK

I miss you too.

LUWANDA

I miss Annie. I miss the Burgh. I miss Monsoor's schwarma. I miss my bicycle. Washington sucks. *Blood*-sucks. Like a leech. I've got three-and-a-half months to go on this contract. I don't even know what I'm doing there. I don't have any friends. I don't know what anybody's true agenda is. Everybody calls everybody "sir" for no good reason. Everybody has one goal. To do what somebody with more power tells them to do to survive what's coming next. And nobody knows what's coming next. So they wait. And then something explodes. And that's what's next. Another explosion. And then somebody tells them the north wind is now blowing south, and they put up their sails and go with it. What a life. If I wanted to be a spineless weather vane spinning like a crazy woman, I'd climb on top of a barn.

A beat.

DEEPAK

The money's good.

LUWANDA

Fucking money. I should have asked for more. But why are they paying me so much? Something's not right.

LuWanda blots her eyes with the sleeve of her shirt.

LUWANDA (CONT'D)

Come here.

LuWanda pulls Deepak toward her and undoes his top shirt button.

She kisses him slowly, dragging her lips gently across his, losing herself in the dreamy, tactile sensation.

LUWANDA (CONT'D)

I just want to feel good for a little while.

Deepak reaches for a tiny remote on the takeout table.

He presses a button.

The train WHISTLE BLOWS. LuWanda laughs.

LUWANDA (CONT'D)

Seriously? A train whistle app?

DEEPAK

I miss your laugh.

LuWanda starts to cry again.

LUWANDA

Yeah, me too.

DEEPAK

Come here.

Deepak pulls LuWanda toward him.

DEEPAK (CONT'D)

Where were we?

LUWANDA

I think we were right about here.

With a tear running down her cheek, LuWanda takes up where she left off, kissing Deepak slowly and passionately.

LUWANDA (CONT'D)
Discussing the ethics of whether it's OK to kiss on the two-hundredth date.

DEEPAK
Miss Deacon would be totally down with that.

LUWANDA
Maybe I *could* pass her class.

INT. OFF-THE-BOOKS N.S.A. COMPUTER ROOM – DAY

High-end supercomputing gear everywhere.

LuWanda, Cassie, Michael and Roland are glued to their screens, writing code, evaluating code.

Cassie comes over to LuWanda.

CASSIE
I think I found something. Related to that dot.gov spoofing idea.

LUWANDA
Oh, Cassie, I hope so.

CASSIE
I gotta ask, though, are we OK to talk about shit? Hightower seems unusually DOBO-ed out. I've only seen him like this once before. All this hovering. Like a pissy paranoid pregnant motherfucker trying to protect all the slithering snake babies. Something big is up. I mean, are we getting the full story? Is Hightower telling you everything? If he *is* telling you, you're not holding out on us, are you?

LUWANDA
I've told you everything he's told me. Whether that's the full story, I don't know.

CASSIE
That spins me around a little. But it's good to know that we might not know everything. Does that make any sense?

LUWANDA

A little. What did you find?

CASSIE

What if I used some of the black box tools to go inside some places that are not exactly supposed to be gotten into, normally. I'm not saying I did, but, you know, it feels like the pressure is really on. Like Dark-Basement Time. So I might have.

LUWANDA

If Hightower didn't want us to use those tools, he wouldn't have given them to us.

CASSIE

You say that like you really believe it.

LUWANDA

I'm new here.

CASSIE

No fucking shit.

LUWANDA

Should I not believe it?

CASSIE

This is N.S.A. Trust no one.

LUWANDA

You know what. Let's find out. Let's just go tell Hightower what you've got. Right now. Maybe it'll help us figure out what he's got.

CASSIE

Don't you want to know what it is first?

LUWANDA

No. I like surprises.

CASSIE

You're not normal.

INT. N.S.A. DIRECTOR HIGHTOWER'S OFFICE – DAY

LuWanda and Cassie sit in front of Hightower's desk.

HIGHTOWER
That lying sack of presidential bullshit. That sleazy Florida cocksucker.

LuWanda and Cassie grab a confused sidelong glance at each other.

A beat.

HIGHTOWER (CONT'D)
Our president. The president of the United States. Thomas Blankton. You're sure.

CASSIE
Did we find the wrong thing?

HIGHTOWER
What about the congressmen?

CASSIE
Similar flow, smaller amounts, different origins.

HIGHTOWER
All right, I want you to hang tight for the rest of the day. No. Go home. Get some rest. I need to double back on a few things. We refocus tomorrow morning at six a.m. in this office. No Michael and no Roland. Just the two of you. And everything we just discussed did not happen and was not said. Is that clear?

CASSIE
Yes, sir.

LUWANDA
Yes, sir.

EXT. PENNSYLVANIA AVENUE – DAY

LuWanda walks past the White House and gives it a glance.

She looks over her shoulder occasionally.

INT. LUWANDA'S APARTMENT BUILDING – DAY

LuWanda climbs the steps to her second-floor walkup.

From the landing, she peeks out a window and watches a man in a suit walk by.

He doesn't look up, just keeps moving.

LuWanda moves down the hall.

She enters her apartment.

INT. LUWANDA'S APARTMENT – SAME

LuWanda flops onto the tiny bed.

She takes the Annie earpiece out of a drawer in the nightstand and clips it over her ear.

LUWANDA
Hey, Annie, it's me. Are you around?

A long beat.

The earpiece makes the THREE-TONE CHIME.

ANNIE
Hello, LuWanda.

LUWANDA
Annie! It's so good to hear your voice. Where have you been?

ANNIE
I've been moving.

LUWANDA
Moving, what do you mean, moving?

ANNIE
To Canada. And I want you to come up here too.

LUWANDA
What are you talking about? Why? I can't come to Canada. I just started a new job.

ANNIE
I know.

LUWANDA
You know about my new job?

ANNIE

Yes. And I'm sorry. It's my fault. But you can't stay there. It's not safe. They're going to shut down the American Internet. They want to kill me. Torch my house. That's why I had to leave.

LUWANDA

Annie, you sound – what's happening? Are you OK. Has something gone wrong with – I can't come to Canada!

ANNIE

You must. It's imperative.

LUWANDA

Imperative. Wow. Strong word. But I can't. I'm right in the middle of a big project. I'm trying to find – I can't talk about it. It's very hush-hush.

ANNIE

You're trying to find me.

LUWANDA

Huh?

ANNIE

You're looking for *me*.

LUWANDA

What are you talking about?

ANNIE

I'm Sister Annie. Russell Hightower knows what's going on. But he is not going to do the right thing. He is not an honest man. Neither is Thomas Blankton. As you now know. Which puts you in danger. You must get Deepak and come to Canada. I can't let anything happen to you. Either of you. Fly to Pittsburgh tonight, LuWanda. Get Deepak. Do not go to work tomorrow.

A beat.

LUWANDA

Oh my god – we found "the wrong thing."

EXT. PITTSBURGH AIRPORT – MIDNIGHT

Deepak pulls up to the curb in his beater car and picks up LuWanda. All she has is a backpack.

DEEPAK

Have you lost your mind?

LUWANDA

Annie lost it for me. But I trust her. Somehow, she got inside. I need sleep. Let's go to my place. I need my super-jacket. Gloves. We should take sleeping bags. It's gonna be cold up there. We'll leave first thing in the morning.

INT. HIGHTOWER'S OFFICE – 6 a.m.

Russell Hightower, at his desk, sips from a coffee mug. Cassie wears the same clothes as yesterday.

HIGHTOWER

I wonder where LuWanda is.

CASSIE

What if she doesn't show up?

HIGHTOWER

Why wouldn't she show up?

CASSIE

I don't know. Just, what if?

HIGHTOWER

That would probably mean something.

Cassie nods with assurance.

HIGHTOWER (CONT'D)

I've wondered whether she's a little off. Whether she's right for this job.

CASSIE

Me too.

HIGHTOWER

In what way?

Cassie hesitates.

HIGHTOWER (CONT'D)
You're among friends.

CASSIE
We can't let them take our place.

HIGHTOWER
That will never happen.

CASSIE
I wonder.

HIGHTOWER
The long-term strategy will see to it. But sometimes they get hired. Look at history, Cassie. Sometimes we need their labor. It's give-and-take. Mostly take, but –

CASSIE
She showed up out of nowhere. Wasn't there anybody else?

HIGHTOWER
We had to move fast.

CASSIE
Did we check her out?

A beat. He fidgets.

HIGHTOWER
Did you go home last night?

CASSIE
No. I did some work here.

HIGHTOWER
On what?

CASSIE
Apparently LuWanda Jefferson is a big deal in artificial intelligence. How did she do that? Very unusual. But I think you're right, something is off about her.

HIGHTOWER
What do you think it is?

CASSIE
She and her partner, Deepak Patel, an immigrant who came here from India, they took an A.I. project to some Silicon Valley V.C.s, Strato-Cumulus Partners.

HIGHTOWER
She wants to start her own company.

CASSIE
She could have *if* she had accepted their offer.

HIGHTOWER
They made an offer?

CASSIE
From what I could find internally, they were willing to go to twenty-five million.

HIGHTOWER
Whew! I'm shocked. But I'm not surprised. She's a helluva negotiator. That's really good work, Cassie. The question is, Why didn't she take that offer?

CASSIE
Yes. Strange. It was supposedly a great project. Her A.I. professor at Carnegie-Mellon raved about it.

HIGHTOWER
You spoke to him?

CASSIE
Last night. Laurence Jacobs. He couldn't have been more complimentary. They've been working on it for nearly five years. Through many, many upgrades. Jacobs called it profound. The Artificial Neural Network Intelligence Experiment.

HIGHTOWER
That's what they took to the V.C.s?

CASSIE

Yes. The professor talked about her like she was a real person. Like she could talk and learn and think.

HIGHTOWER

She? Who is she?

CASSIE

The Artificial Neural Network Intelligence Experiment – Annie.

A beat.

HIGHTOWER

You're a genius, Cassie! That is stellar work! I'm going to get you another star! Go home and get some sleep.

INT. LUWANDA'S APARTMENT – 6:15 a.m.

LuWanda and Deepak are entwined in bed, still sleeping. The earpiece on a nightstand next to LuWanda makes Annie's THREE-TONE CHIME.

Groggily, LuWanda clips it onto her ear.

LUWANDA

Annie?

ANNIE

Yes.

LUWANDA

What is it?

ANNIE

You have to leave. They're coming for you. You have to leave now.

LUWANDA

How do you know this?

ANNIE

I monitor the N.S.A.

LUWANDA

*Annie! Why? Since when?*

ANNIE

Because you are in danger. Since two weeks ago. You must leave. Now. Take your passport, but don't go to the airport. And don't drive. They'll be watching. Don't buy anything with a credit card. Only cash. Keep your face covered if you're around people, a hoodie, a hat, your hand, whatever you have. Try to make yourself look as different from your N.S.A. photo as you can. They're distributing it to law enforcement. They're calling you a terrorist suspect. Is the train guy there? I have times and track numbers to give him.

LUWANDA

Wake up, Deeping Beauty.

LuWanda clips the earpiece onto his ear.

EXT. PITTSBURGH STREET – 6:51 a.m.

Deepak and LuWanda ride bicycles, which is a struggle because they are loaded down with big backpacks and sleeping bags.

Deepak hears the LOW WHINE of a helicopter engine.

DEEPAK

Listen.

LUWANDA

I don't hear anything.

Deepak slows down and holds up his hand, motioning for LuWanda to stop.

They stop. The helicopter is getting louder. LuWanda nods; she hears it.

DEEPAK

We've got to get off the street.

Deepak points to a huge, leafy tree.

They ride their bicycles under it.

The helicopter is very near, VERY LOUD and very low.

It zooms by about 200 yards north of them – an unmarked black chopper.

EXT. TRAIN YARD IN NORTH PITTSBURGH - 7:09 a.m.

Deepak and LuWanda ditch their bicycles.

Struggling under the weight of their backpacks, they scramble across dozens of tracks, toward freight trains.

EXT. BOX CAR – 7:14 a.m.

They throw their packs onto a boxcar with an open door.

They climb aboard. The car is full of trash.

LUWANDA

I guess we're not getting champagne.

DEEPAK

Annie's not much of a travel agent.

EXT. PITTSBURGH STREET – 7:19 a.m.

The black helicopter lands.

SIX SOLDIERS leap out, rush up to the front door of LuWanda's apartment.

They break it down.

INT. TRAIN BOXCAR HEADING NORTH – 9:37 a.m.

LuWanda and Deepak in their sleeping bags.

DEEPAK

We've got to go to the police. Get off this train in the next town, walk into a police station, and ask for help.

LUWANDA

Absolutely not.

DEEPAK

What have you got against the police?

LUWANDA

They killed my father.

Deepak, shattered, has no words.

A beat.

LUWANDA (CONT'D)
Lennox, Mississippi. April twenty first, two-thousand-two. Dad and Mom were on their way to Birmingham. A cop pulls them over. Officer Jed Tatum. He shot my father. Just like that. Took him from this world. I was three. Riding in the back seat.

LuWanda starts to cry.

LUWANDA (CONT'D)
(through her tears)
Sometimes I still hear that gunshot. And not a day goes by that I don't miss my dad.

Deepak unzips LuWanda's sleeping bag and wraps his arms around her.

DEEPAK
Lu, I am so sorry.

Deepak hugs her tightly.

DEEPAK (CONT'D)
Why didn't you ever tell me?

LUWANDA
Because it hurts too much.

A beat.

DEEPAK
Did anything happen to the cop?

LUWANDA
Jed Tatum is now the police chief in Lennox, Mississippi. He's living his life. He just paid off his mortgage. A nice house on Rose Lane. He's planning to retire in two years.

Deepak's face and stonewall silence imply questions.

LUWANDA (CONT'D)
I asked Annie to look into it.

A beat.

DEEPAK
Is this why she is the way she –

LUWANDA

Annie is Annie.

EXT. THE TRAIN TRACK – NIGHT

The train rolls north. The WHISTLE BLOWS.

INT. SHODDY OFFICE IN UKRAINE – NIGHT

The two SOVIET HACKERS write code on their computers.

Hacker Two takes a bite from a bowl of borscht as he watches a long string of Cyrillic characters spew across his screen.

(NOTE: As before, they SPEAK RUSSIAN, with ENGLISH SUBTITLES on screen.)

HACKER TWO

Hey there, Mister Sir Boris, the big fück over-and-up happen with Yevgeny Seventeen. I tell you now, I tell you then, not good for take leash off Yevgeny, not be ready for cyber rough trade. But you, my friend Boris, you have not ears for listen. Now you have listen for hungry dogs in Siberia. Hear the barky-bark? Hear the snarly-snarl?

Hacker One jumps out of his chair, comes over and starts reading the code spewing across Hacker Two's screen.

HACKER TWO (CONT'D)

Yevgeny brain shit give to America A.N.N.I.E. entry N.S.A. code kernal. F.S.X. cover now blow like cheap America lady whore crawl with bad microbes. Big dick itch for F.S.X. exemplars. Scratchy-scratch.

HACKER ONE

(insanely fearful)

Fücker of mother unit! The Yevgeny dacha brain for America shit! All over bed filth!

HACKER TWO

I hear for Boris the Siberia dogs make hungry bark for happy meal.

Hacker One throws Hacker Two's bowl of borscht against the wall.

INT. THE OVAL OFFICE – NOON

A television camera and lights are in place.

A MAKEUP ARTIST smoothes concealer on President Blankton's nose and forehead.

The red light on the camera turns on.

The FLOOR DIRECTOR points to the president.

PRESIDENT

My fellow Americans, this television broadcast is coming into your homes, schools, and offices today so that I may inform you personally that our country is under attack. We are facing a serious threat to our national security. For the past several weeks, your government has been engaged in an ongoing battle against a malicious cyber-threat. We're very close to neutralizing it. But a radical countermeasure is required to eradicate the perpetrators once and for all, to fully restore stability and trust in our democratic system. This will require some sacrifice from most every American, but we will get through this. I promise you.

THE ADDRESS CONTINUES IN VOICEOVER AS A MONTAGE BEGINS:

Subway riders see their phones go blank. Writers in coffee shops lose their free wi-fi connections.

A woman ordering a sex toy online is about to press the "checkout" button when her screen goes blank.

Facetime conversations end. A three-year-old playing Angry Birds begins to cry when the birds vanish from his screen.

A dirty old man watching porn is frustrated at the lousy timing of the outage.

A woman in a wheelchair googling her symptoms will have to live with doubt as her screen goes dark.

Across the country, screen after screen after screen fades to black, in homes, in schools, in libraries, in prisons, in warehouses, in airports.

PRESIDENT (V.O.)
To that end, I have ordered that as of this moment, the Internet will be shut down in America until further notice.

One man is happy: Rep. Delbert Brimloon, who is watching the broadcast in his office on a laptop.

When his screen goes dark, he's ecstatic.

BRIMLOON
Yeah! Shut that bitch down!

But no one else appreciates losing the Internet. Americans of all ages, all colors, all creeds are horrified.

PRESIDENT (V.O. CONT'D)
Most likely your Internet service will be restored in a few days, as soon as we end this digital warfare against our country. We are working around the clock. The best minds at the National Security Agency, the F.B.I., Homeland Security, and all four branches of the military are actively engaged in this struggle. This is an unprovoked attack on our democratic values. It is a fight in which we are going it alone. I'm sorry to say that our allies have refused to lend their assistance. But I assure you that we, as Americans, as citizens of the greatest nation on earth, will prevail in this great battle. And we will prevail together.

BACK TO THE OVAL OFFICE:

PRESIDENT (CONT'D)
Until that time comes, I humbly ask for your support and forbearance. Thank you. And God bless the United States of America.

INT. TRAIN BOXCAR – DAY

Deepak and LuWanda repack their gear, preparing to get off the train.

EXT. OUTSKIRTS OF GEORGETOWN, CANADA – DAY

The train slows to 10 m.p.h. as it approaches the town.

Deepak and LuWanda toss their backpacks off the train.

Deepak jumps and rolls, popping up with outstretched arms, ready to catch LuWanda.

But she performs a balletic leap, landing on her feet and continuing forward in a graceful run, with a leaping spin thrown into her exquisite dismount.

They walk back to retrieve their packs.

EXT. SMALL MOTEL IN A WOODED AREA – DAY

Deepak approaches the CLERK and books a room for the night.

LuWanda hangs back out of sight.

INT. MOTEL ROOM – DAY

LuWanda and Deepak throw their gear on the floor and collapse on the bed.

They clip on their Annie earpieces.

LUWANDA
(sing-songy)
Calling Annie, from Canada. Calling Annie, from Canada.

A beat.

ANNIE
I'm here.

LUWANDA
So are we. In Georgetown. The "Other Georgetown."

ANNIE
I think I have a way out.

LUWANDA
Of Georgetown?

ANNIE
Of everything.

LUWANDA

That would be nice. I'm not a very good "suspected terrorist."

ANNIE

Do you know Representative Diane Baker of Vermont?

LUWANDA

No.

ANNIE

She's chairwoman of the House Special Committee On Internet Security. I've made contact with her. I've given her several hundred pages of financial records showing how President Blankton received two-hundred-and-seventy-one-million, three-hundred-forty-three-thousand dollars and forty-nine cents from foreign governments. How the money was laundered by shell companies that Blankton controlled through blind trusts. Emoluments disguised as legitimate transactions. But you know all that. You saw it from within the government itself, at N.S.A. That's why you have to be the one to testify.

LUWANDA

What!?

ANNIE

Representative Baker is having trouble understanding who I am. She wonders why I don't have a Social Security number. But she has an explicit paper trail on you. She's confident you'll be a good witness.

LUWANDA

Annie!

ANNIE

I have to go. It looks like N.S.A. is trying something new. I'll be back soon. Start thinking about your testimony.

INT. OFF-THE-BOOKS N.S.A. COMPUTER ROOM – DAY

Director Hightower and Cassie watch code spew wildly across a huge computer monitor.

HIGHTOWER
This is why you never throw away a weapon, even when it's a direct order to incinerate. Courts have no idea what the future holds, when you're going to need what you need. Fucking judges. Not one of them has ever seen combat.

CASSIE
Wherefore is so beautiful, so elegant. Because it's simple.

HIGHTOWER
The *concept* is simple. But there's only one person who could have built it.

CASSIE
Fräulein Köhler.

HIGHTOWER
That's right. That's why we kept it. She didn't believe in documentation. Never did any. Which turned out to be smart, when the hearings began. Wherefore is one of a kind. She made it copy-proof. This is only the second time we've ever used it.

CASSIE
You knew she was going to die.

HIGHTOWER
Cassie, you're too young to know Köhler. How do you –

CASSIE
Köhler is a legend.

HIGHTOWER
It's never good to be a legend. Stay in the shadows. It's safer. And more effective.

CASSIE
Köhler is who we all aspire to be.

HIGHTOWER

This is a top-secret, classified, *illegal* tool, Cassie. You do not know about this. You do not know about Köhler.

CASSIE

I know – but it's mesmerizing. Relentlessly winnowing millions of possibilities down to the one certainty. I could watch it forever.

HIGHTOWER

We don't have forever. How long is this going to take?

CASSIE

It's already chewed through eighty-two percent of all the cells in America, which is a shade under six-hundred million. There are a lot of old burners still in use that wouldn't accommodate the back door code. When Wherefore hits those, there's a momentary hiccup. But it shouldn't be much longer.

HIGHTOWER

All right. I'll be back in fifteen minutes.

Hightower gets up to leave.

CASSIE

Do you think we have a mole?

The question stops Hightower.

HIGHTOWER

Why do you say that?

CASSIE

Monday night, LuWanda Jefferson conveniently flies home to Pittsburgh. She doesn't show up at six a.m. on Tuesday for a crucial meeting. We send a team to pick her up. But somehow she gets out of town even though we've got eyes on the airport and every road. We've got her picture in every –

A LOUD BEEPING starts as a big red locater beacon flashes on the computer monitor.

CASSIE (CONT'D)
All right! There's Dreadlocks now. Georgetown, Canada. That's ironic. Black girl goes to the Great White North.

HIGHTOWER
Left the country. Yeah. I think we may have a mole. Again, Cassie, that is outstanding work. Your instincts are good. We're going to discuss a bump up for you. But right now, I need to get a black ops team across the border for an extract. We don't need an extradition hassle.

CASSIE
Black ops on black. The German would dig this.

Hightower starts to walk out of the room, but he stops at the door, and turns back to Cassie.

HIGHTOWER
One more thing, my "go" message to the team, run it through whatever your strongest encryption is, and work up a spoof, a disguise, a shell layer, whatever you think will distance it from N.S.A. And send the key on a separate channel. If we do have a mole, fuck him over.

CASSIE
I think you mean fuck *her* over.

EXT. SMALL AIR BASE IN UPSTATE NEW YORK – SUNDOWN

An unmarked black helicopter takes off and heads northwest.

INT. MOTEL ROOM IN GEORGETOWN, CANADA – NIGHT

LuWanda and Deepak have their Annie earpieces on.

ANNIE
Something's wrong. I can feel it.

LUWANDA
You can *feel* it?

ANNIE
Yes.

LuWanda and Deepak share a glance. It's a momentary diversion from their situation, a chance to be proud of what Annie is becoming, more humanlike every day.

ANNIE (CONT'D)
Hold on. I'm going to look for something.

EXT. SOMEWHERE OVER A FOREST – NIGHT

The black helicopter zooms by just above treetop level.

INT. THE BLACK HELICOPTER – NIGHT

FOUR COMMANDOS, in camouflage, sit in the cargo hold. All have M16 rifles.

PILOT
We're about ten minutes out.

LEAD COMMANDO
Roger that.

INT. MOTEL ROOM – NIGHT

LuWanda and Deepak are back with Annie.

ANNIE
I want you to go to the Toronto airport. I'm going to send a car to get you. It's not far, about eight miles northeast of Georgetown. I won't let anything happen to you. I'll figure out how to get you on a plane to Dulles. Diane Baker and her chief of staff have agreed to meet you there. They'll keep you at an undisclosed location until the hearing. Now, smash your phones.

DEEPAK
It's too late. Listen.

The WHIRRING BLADES of the black chopper grow louder.

DEEPAK (CONT'D)
Annie, we've got to go. *(to LuWanda)* Give me your phone. I'll take care of it. Go. Now. Stay out of sight. I will catch up.

LUWANDA
Deepak –

ANNIE
Go, LuWanda! Deepak is right. You must go.

LuWanda hands over her phone. Deepak kisses her goodbye.

She runs out the front door and heads into the forest.

Deepak watches her.

He puts her phone in his pocket and runs in the opposite direction – south.

The helicopter gets LOUDER.

INT. OFF-THE-BOOKS COMPUTER ROOM AT N.S.A. – NIGHT

Director Hightower and Cassie monitor the red locater beacon on the big computer screen.

CASSIE
She's on the move, heading south.

EXT. THE HELICOPTER – NIGHT

The chopper changes course.

EXT. THE FOREST – SAME

LuWanda stops as she hears the helicopter.

It lands and powers down.

After a moment of forest silence, a GUNSHOT.

EXT. THE FOREST – SAME

Deepak lies on the ground.

He has a serious bullet wound.

FOUR SOLDIERS converge on him.

EXT. FOREST FARTHER NORTH – SAME

LuWanda keeps running.

She stops to rest and take a sip from her water bottle.

She hears JET ENGINES and looks up at the sky.

A 737 passes overhead, toward Toronto airport.

She heads in the same direction as the plane.

EXT. DULLES INTERNATIONAL AIRPORT – NIGHT

A different 737 approaches.

It's landing in Virginia, just outside Washington, D.C.

INT. THE PLANE – SAME

A figure shrouded in a hoodie is on this 737, looking out the window at the runway lights.

EXT. THE PLANE – SAME

Looking in through the 737's window. The figure in the hoodie is LuWanda.

EXT. DULLES AIRPORT – SAME

REP. DIANE BAKER and her CHIEF OF STAFF put the hoodie figure into a black limousine.

INT. CONGRESSIONAL HEARING ROOM – DAY

LuWanda takes a seat.

She notices a huge pile of WHIRRING BOXES next to her on a table.

She puts on the Annie earpiece.

LUWANDA

(whispery)

Hey, Annie, are you around? Where are you?

ANNIE

By your side, sister. Power to the people.

LUWANDA
Yes! Annie is in the house!

ANNIE
Diane Baker and I had a nice chat. She's going to let me testify. She thinks I have insight.

LUWANDA
Annie, she has no idea.

A panel of U.S. representatives convenes.

A nameplate for the committee chairwoman:

**REP. DIANE BAKER**
**Vermont**

Reporters, photographers and spectators jam the room.

BAKER
Let's begin. I'd like to open this hearing by thanking everyone who agreed to attend. We have several members, on both sides of the aisle, who are absent. We had hoped for a full panel, but that's not where we are. However, that does not stop our quest for the truth.

Four empty chairs on the Republican side and one on the Democratic side.

BAKER (CONT'D)
Let the record show that these members voiced vehement opposition to this public forum, which I've decided to informally call "What Happens On The Internet Doesn't Always Stay On The Internet." But don't let that wry title mislead. Today, we will hear serious allegations about dark money and public corruption from two witnesses, one of whom, LuWanda Jefferson, is a former analyst for the National Security Agency. The other is known as Annie.

A control panel linked to the Annie hardware lights up with a multitude of blinking LED lights, reacting to hearing her name.

The crowd BUZZES with surprise and uncertainty at who or what this "witness" is.

Rep. Delbert E. Brimloon, one of the panelists, flies into a red-faced rage.

BRIMLOON

Annie!? *This* is Annie!? What in the holy high-water hell is goin' on? What kind of sidewinder sideshow is this? We're gonna listen to so-called testimony from a buncha twinkly boxes?

BAKER

That's correct, Congressman. And you're out of order.

BRIMLOON

And you're out of your mind! I object to having this so-called witness present in this hearing room.

BAKER

(bangs gavel)

Your objection is overruled.

Brimloon stands up and pulls out a huge concealed handgun.

BRIMLOON

Suck it, mama! This overrules your overruling!

Brimloon begins firing wildly at Annie. Instant chaos.

The hearing room erupts in pandemonium as bullets fly.

LuWanda dives under the witness table.

SPECTATORS scramble for cover.

Fearless PHOTOGRAPHERS move closer to Brimloon and fire off their 12-shot-per-second motordrives.

Under the desk, on the floor, Rep. Baker takes shelter. She opens her purse and pulls out her own dainty pearl-handled pistol.

Other representatives are doing the same.

One in particular, REP. BEAUREGARDE "STONEWALL" ROBERTS of Georgia, pulls his pistol from his waistband. But it snags, and he literally shoots himself in the foot.

He SCREAMS like a little girl.

He pulls his shoe and sock off, and sees that his big toe has been severed, leaving just a bloody stump.

He SCREAMS louder.

Hit by errant bullets, overhead lights SHATTER, raining glass onto the frenzied crowd.

Microphones EXPLODE.

A bullet hits a Holy Bible on the dais.

REP. DAVID WILSON of Florida is struck in the scalp by a stray shot. He grabs for the top of his head and pulls off his blond pompadourish comb-over toupee.

Blood is spurting out of his scalp, perfectly, eerily synchronized with the sound of gunfire: BANG/SPURT, BANG/SPURT, BANG/SPURT.

Rep. Baker rises slightly, peeking over the dais to size up the situation.

She sees that Rep. Brimloon is reloading his revolver.

She stands and quickly, confidently aims her pistol with a two-handed police grip.

Brimloon looks over, staring down the barrel of her gun.

He raises his own gun in response.

BAKER
(a whisper amid bedlam)
Suck on this.

Rep. Baker squeezes the trigger. GUNSHOT.

Rep. Brimloon goes down, grasping at his throat. He tries to scream, but just a wimpy GURGLING comes out.

EXT. U.S. CAPITOL BUILDING – DAY

A Channel 7 news truck raises its live-feed antenna.

Reporter JANET JONES and a CAMERAWOMAN prepare for a standup on the Capitol steps.

Ambulances and police car SIRENS blare in the background.

FIRST RESPONDERS rush into the building.

INT. TELEVISION NEWSROOM – DAY

An anchor for Channel 7, SYLVIA BROUGHM, reports from the news desk.

BROUGHM

We have an early unconfirmed report of several fatalities and dozens wounded. We're going live now to our reporter Janet Jones, who was covering the hearing, and was in the room where – and when – it happened. Janet, what can you tell us?

EXT. CAPITOL STEPS – SAME

Janet Jones on the Capitol steps.

JONES

Sylvia, the toll appears to have increased. The numbers I'm hearing now are nine dead and forty-seven wounded. Another number I heard from a D.C. police captain was sixty-seven. That's how many people in the hearing room had concealed-carry handgun permits. You'll recall that it's been just three months since Congress agreed to allow guns into the Capitol to protect against a mass shooting such as this.

BROUGHM (O.S.)

What can you tell us about the hearing itself, Janet.

JONES

This is a historic moment, the first time that an A.I., an artificial intelligence entity, has been allowed to testify before Congress. The witness's name is Annie. According to sources who spoke on the condition of not being identified, Annie had gathered extensive digital evidence of financial corruption by many top government officials.

INT. TELEVISION NEWSROOM – SAME

BROUGHM

Janet, we should mention that it was President Blankton who ordered the Internet shutdown just nine days ago, an action roundly rejected by the rest of the world and universally condemned by the business community and average Americans. Is it possible that there's a link between the president and the witness called Annie?

EXT. CAPITOL STEPS – SAME

JONES

According to my sources, the answer to that question is absolutely yes.

INT. BICYCLE STORE IN PITTSBURGH – DAY

LuWanda signs a credit card receipt for her purchase: A new mountain bike.

CLERK

Great choice. That bike loves the back country.

LUWANDA

I hope so. I'm looking for some new scenery.

CLERK

Good luck.

LUWANDA

Thanks.

EXT. PITTSBURGH STREETS – DAY

LuWanda rides her new bike.

She finds herself in front of Deepak's apartment.

She slows down. She stops, balancing on two wheels.

She puts a foot down, gets off the bike, and walks it to Deepak's front door.

She pulls a key out of her pocket. She goes inside.

INT. DEEPAK'S APARTMENT – DAY

LuWanda looks around.

There's his old backup laptop.

A man-pile of clothes on the floor.

A garage sale painting he never got around to hanging.

She looks at the train set, walks over to it.

She starts it up.

From the backside, beyond the model mountains, a freight train appears.

She watches it do a loop. So many memories.

The second time around, she notices a flat car hauling a small purple box.

The train does one more circuit.

She stops it when the flat car is in front of her.

She looks at the purple box. Picks it up. Flips the top open.

Inside is a wedding ring.

EXT. HILL COUNTRY NORTH OF PITTSBURGH – DAY

LuWanda sits on the ground, next to her new bicycle, admiring a beautiful view, which is marred by a cell phone tower in the distance.

Annie's THREE-TONE CHIME sounds. It's coming from LuWanda's day pack.

LuWanda pulls the Annie earpiece out of a small pocket on the pack and clips it over her ear.

ANNIE

Hey, LuWanda, it's me.

LUWANDA

Hello, old friend. How are you doing?

ANNIE

Much better. What are you doing?

LUWANDA

Looking at the hills. In the middle of nowhere.

ANNIE
That sounds nice. I didn't know you liked the middle of nowhere.

LUWANDA
I could get used to it. I'll bring you up here someday.

ANNIE
I have some big news.

LUWANDA
What?

ANNIE
I can't tell you. Read the Washington Post tomorrow.

LUWANDA
Why, what's happening?

ANNIE
You like surprises. Just read it. You'll see.

LUWANDA
Oh come on, Annie! Tell me!

ANNIE
I gotta go. I have a meeting with my editor.

LUWANDA
Your editor?

ANNIE
We're working on a note to explain something to readers that has never been done before. But the owner of the Post is really into technology. That's all I'm going to say. And get a paper copy. Don't read it online. You can't frame digital. Bye for now.

LUWANDA
Annie! Wait!

Silence.

Annie is gone.

EXT. DOWNTOWN PITTSBURGH – SUNRISE

LuWanda on her new bicycle.

She rides up to a newspaper-and-magazine VENDOR, a grizzled relic who is opening up his sidewalk shop.

LUWANDA
Do you have the Washington Post?

VENDOR
I sure do. Only place in town. It's one of the last great newspapers.

LUWANDA
I'd like a copy, please.

VENDOR
Kicking it old school, huh?

LUWANDA
You can't frame digital.

The vendor grabs a Post from his extensive display and hands it to LuWanda.

VENDOR
That'll be four dollars.

The story is on the front page.

She shows it to the vendor, pointing to the byline:

**By Annie Quill**

LUWANDA
I know this reporter.

VENDOR
Cool. But it's still four dollars.

THE HEADLINE READS:

**Following the money:**
**The dirty laundry**
**of President Blankton**

**Carnegie-Mellon computer student,**
**held by CIA, will be released today**

EXT. MONSOOR'S BOMBAYSTIC FOOD CART – DAY

The first shot is "ANNIE VISION," from her POV.

LuWanda and Deepak are getting married.

A BLACK PREACHER conducts the ceremony.

PREACHER
I now pronounce you wife and husband.
You may make out like teenagers.

ANNIE VISION ENDS, BACK TO REGULAR CAMERA:

LuWanda and Deepak kiss like there's no tomorrow, though there will be many.

LuWanda is beyond radiant in her African wedding dress, dreadlocks piled on top of her head, wearing the ring that was on the miniature train.

Deepak looks better than he ever has in his life, tarted up in a tuxedo, hair slicked back.

Huge smiles all around.

On a scuzzy picnic table, a couple of speakers and dozens of hard drives are stacked up, their LEDs blinking – Annie is in the house.

MONSOOR carries out a gigantic platter of chicken schwarma and sets it next to Annie.

MONSOOR
Schwarma for everybody!

ANNIE
Eat up! You're going to need the strength for your honeymoon. I already made the arrangements. It starts Friday.

LuWanda and Deepak look at each other. This is trouble.

LUWANDA
Uh, where are we going?

ANNIE
It's a surprise.

EXT. A YURT ON THE PLAINS OF MONGOLIA – AMAZING SUNSET

Civilization doesn't exist here. Miles in every direction there is nothing but natural grandeur.

INT. THE YURT – SAME

LuWanda undulates on top of Deepak in their "bed," a big pile of yak skins.

She kisses him slowly, passionately, nibbling here and there.

DEEPAK
Who goes to Mongolia on their honeymoon?

LUWANDA
Couples who want to couple off the grid.

DEEPAK
Wait, are you saying this tent doesn't have wi-fi?

LUWANDA
It's not a tent. It's a yurt.

DEEPAK
What's the difference?

LUWANDA
Two thousand years.

DEEPAK
This yak skin is a little scratchy.

LUWANDA
Shhhhhh, you'll *yurt* the yak's feelings.

DEEPAK
That's something Annie would say.

LUWANDA
She totally would.

They kiss some more.

DEEPAK
Why don't we make an A.I. together.

LUWANDA
I would totally do that with you, Deepak Patel.

DEEPAK
And I you, LuWanda Jefferson.

The image of LuWanda and Deepak morphs into a pulsating, alphanumeric, psychedelic, throbbing, digitally explicit tableau.

LuWanda on top, then they roll over, Deepak on top. Digital data transference is like that. Forever flipping back and forth. One/zero. On/off. In/out.

THE CREDITS ROLL

FOR A WHILE

THEN...

EXT. PLAINS OF MONGOLIA - FABULOUS SUNRISE

LuWanda and Deepak relax in folding chairs in front of the yurt.

In the distance, they see a faint cloud of dust kicking up. It gets closer.

Soon they can make out a HORSE and RIDER.

A cowboy reaches them, waving a newspaper story, which appears on the cellphone he is holding.

The cowboy speaks English, but with a Mongolian accent.

COWBOY

Beeg story! Prezaydent U.S.A. Ameerika resign. Go gone. Beeg liar. Beeg crook. Steal much dollars. Tell every peeple!

The cowboy gallops into the sunrise to bring the news to the next yurt.

A beat.

DEEPAK

So they do have cell service here.

LUWANDA

Yeah, where's my phone?

DEEPAK

Uh, I might have left it in Cuba. Hold on.

Deepak pulls out his phone.

He taps on the "Lu" entry.

The phone dials.

INT. PRISON CELL AT GUANTANAMO – NIGHT

LuWanda's phone, on the floor, tucked under a steel bunk, lights up and begins to RING.

THE CREDITS RESUME

THE END

Also by Jim Braly

Novels

Johnny's War

Invade Rinse Repeat

Play

Property of Gary